Ŗ

Anna Vaught is an English teacher, mentor and author of several books, including 2020's *Saving Lucia* and *Famished*. Her memoir, *These Envoys of Beauty*, will be published by Reflex in 2023, followed by a novel, *The Zebra and Lord Jones*, from Renard Press. Her work is published in journals, anthologies and the national press, and she was a monthly columnist for *The Bookseller*. She is a guest university lecturer, speaks at literary and arts events and is a tutor for Jericho Writers, also working as a volunteer with young people who need literacy support. Anna is from a large Welsh family and lives in Wiltshire with her American husband and three sons. She works alongside chronic illness and additional caring responsibilities and is passionate about the role of creative work for wellbeing.

RAVISHED

A SERIES OF REFLECTIONS ON AGE, SEX, DEATH, AND JUDGEMENT

ANNA VAUGHT

REFLEX PRESS

First published as a collection in 2022 by Reflex Press
Abingdon, Oxfordshire, OX14 3SY
www.reflex.press

A CIP catalogue record of this book is
available from the British Library.

ISBN: 978-1-914114-10-6

1 3 5 7 9 10 8 6 4 2

Printed and bound in Great Britain by
Severn, Gloucester.

Cover image by Inkling Design

www.reflex.press/ravished/

To all the weirdos – like me – who don't belong.
I love you.

CONTENTS

He Looked Back

Do not do that cursed thing, *oh no*. Do not look back when you feel a little chill or a thread of warmth work its way up this arm and that. If it were me, my glacial ones, my pretty little brass monkeys, I would not look from the corner of my eye on the day you wake up and there's an ache and a purple glow to one side. Then, do not look from the corner of your eye, oh no. Chin up and straight ahead and out of bed you climb, tippety tat on your confident feet; descend the stair to your coffee cup and your victuals and a radio pulsing. Look straight ahead as you leave your house and out into your quotidian. But I can only advise.

Here comes a story of one who should have known better. I heard it had come to a conclusion last Thursday when a light drizzle settled in and, as Berenson – we dispense here with first names; too intimate in a great vault of folk, just commingling as one, I tell you – walked home from an unremarkable job in the city, the darkness began to fall over London in November. From office to tube and from tube to the beginning of his walk home, he was content enough. Even with the grey evening, the drizzle was refreshing on the skin after a day in the office. He observed familiar faces on his way, nods of acknowledgement and, to a certain extent, he fancied, of understanding. The day had gone tolerably well. He thought, though did not ponder long, that it was unseasonably cold.

Walking up the final small spiral staircase from the tube station, though, Berenson was struck with an odd feeling: of the familiar being just a little off beam. He could not put a finger on it, but it made him shudder. Thinking carefully, the white tiles looked perhaps a little yellowing, the steps altogether dustier. Now and then, he felt someone brush against his shoulder, yet he had no sense of someone quite so close to him as he made the final ascent to the street.

Again, he shuddered. He twitched, and there was a pain in one shoulder blade, of a twist round restrained by some instinct, deeply plumbed. He walked on. Footslogging, a little weary, in the direction of home, he stepped first into the everyday sight of a London street with its selection of shops. He bought an evening newspaper, rolled it up and put it under his arm. Again, the shops looked a little different. There was an unseemly and garish quality to the lighting and the bright displays of goods, even in the small newsagents where he stopped every evening. He had never noticed that before, always enjoying the convivial warmth of the shops and shop-keepers as he walked home. The yellow was not soft, nor was it the aggressive neon of the office strip light. 'Dead canary' was the phrase fluttering in his mind now.

He reached the end of the road, where shops began to give way to the residential streets. Berenson had an unusual feeling – almost like the warmth of someone's breath on his back. He shook it off. 'Maybe,' he thought, 'I have one of my heads coming on. I've been working pretty hard.' But the feeling did not abate; it grew stronger and more disconcerting. Now, rounding the corner into his own street, it occurred to Berenson that he had yet to turn round. To have done so would have been to give credence to what he thought a foolish sensation. So, he walked on. But, as he did so, while aware of the possibility of a twist in the spine and whip of the knee, he was conscious of the increasing closeness of another individual and, also, of footsteps behind him. Yet, when he stopped, so did the sensation and the hoof taps. It was true: they did sound very like a shod horse striking a road. Moving on again, walking more quickly, the steps and the individual kept pace with him. Looking around, he had the bizarre sensation that he was seeing everything as it always was – but through a glass darkly. Walk on, walk on. Did he hear a laugh behind him? Feel the flash of cold and the slipping away of his first name. The breath on the shoulder. He was sure of it, and again his shoulder blade pained in an ache to turn round and confront the ridiculous thing. 'One of my heads one of my heads one of my heads.'

Oh, there is terrible panic in repetition and in the silly mantras your warm people employ. It always makes me laugh. Now, Berenson! Was the breathing full and throaty? Of course, it was. I had whispered to you not to turn around, but do you people listen to me or to the other with his cod-warmth and his promises and his baby Jesus picnics? Fools, all. You turned around, did you not? And did the man behind him identify himself as *Berenson* when, unable to bear it anymore, you, Berenson, assuaged the pain in your shoulder blade in turning? *Oh, worse pain. Yes, that fellow carried on in your quotidian and your tippety tap shoes and in your life, your skin, your suit.*

And your mother preferred him.

Daylight saw Berenson travelling, as usual, down a pleasant city street and past shops making brisk trade and on the London underground. All was well. Tonight, no story would appear in his newspaper about the diligent, well-respected man found cold and dead in his street last night. Ah, on. He was here, instead, swept into this coalescence of mine. You did not listen, Berenson! You did not listen to me! And the man who cut him down would, while there was time, sit in Berenson's favourite chair and tweak at what we know of our everyday familiar world. He would shuffle off his steel-tapped shoes, brush a little lint from his fine dark suit. And he would laugh. He's a friend of mine. My friends are manifold, on the surface world, and getting more so. And there's a hecatomb of such folk as you in the cold. None of this was what you expected, any of you.

A Welsh Gravedigger Laments
(or Why It Is Better to Be Dead in Wales)

Merciful heaven!
What, man! ne'er pull your hat upon your brows;
Give sorrow words; the grief that does not speak
Whispers the o'er-fraught heart and bids it break.
—*Macbeth*

The things I have seen. What went missing; what was lost, sometimes unaccountably. And once upon a time, I was not able to give sorrow words. Therefore, it held; I could not cradle it, talk to it and say, 'Hello thing, what can you teach me?' But, you see, I learned, out there, doing the digging, with the wailing and all. That's other people's losses, but there were my own, legion and mostly sticky.

In my younger years, if I'd had the vocabulary, I'd have called the losses (my own, I speak of) aphotic, Stygian in their darkness. But from the corner of my eye, and as the new world of words brewed alongside, I began instead to see them as navy, like a late twilight in indigo, with a little cyan if you screwed up your eyes. Knew that from my paintbox. Soon, if I looked with the whole of my eye, I began to see wisps of lavender light in there. In desolate places and with people who should have cared, but no, I got big on ombre and subtle shifts in hue or pigment. I learned to observe. Just little things, like the turn of a face or a fold in a cushion, but the trappings of a world. In mourning for those who left with explanation, and those whose end was whispered or belied, I grew to usher forth more words as well as that colour, and thus I limned my world. Do you know that the hour of death is a mossy green, sliding into turtle's back? And it was cold, but not arctic, exactly. As for the folds in the cushion, well now, if you gathered the fabric just a little deeper around them, you had the ravines for a miniature me, crevasse for a tiny arthropod. And I found that when I looked at Dead Mammy and Daddy in their coffins, it helped to see the prickly box-fabric as ecru or greige. Bit like them, at that point, if I do not offend.

And now sometimes, I help out old Evans the Bodies (you'll meet him again later, in this good book) up there with his Dead Dears, his corpse friends (again, if I don't offend), and much depends on how you go, see, but never be scared of a human being at full tilt of rest. You see the ecru or the greige, but I tell you that beyond these shades, there is a dark thing, then the twist of a sparkle. I do not know if it's God or the bright face of the baby Jesus; I don't know if it's the pulsing or ruddy mother-hands of Mary. But I tell you that I know, *I know*, there is more, and my God, man, it is a kaleidoscope.

Let me take you back to my child-world, when I was raw colour, like. Yes. As a child, the worlds of dead and living collided; the worlds of truth and the imagination, too. But in their way, these losses were a fair prospect because, by the time I was all grown up, I felt sort of brave in a way that made me some sort of social oddity if I strayed into the wrong company or away from the Welsh plangency that loved the gob, or tang of death and what it yakked.

I learned when to live in an imagination and when to venture out. And there were the colour and the growing word-hoard, treasure box, I told you of.

In darkness, your eyes adjust, don't they? And you see a star, however faint and think, 'Aha, I am a sailor on my bark, and from here I can navigate,' and you imagine yourself aeons back, confronting end times without the day-long tidy terrifying of our news; our always awake technology, screaming, 'Apocalypse!' Still, I might look at that word, even now – apocalypse, not technology, I mean – and wonder at it like new. *Apocalypse*: it's from the ancient Greek, meaning *uncovering*. A word that once had much more celebratory nuances. Word-hoard; colour; etymology, and don't worry there about some fellow thinking you're a weirdy swot. Yes, loss; all the horrid redaction of my growing: its strange way of being. Me on my bark. In the dark. Ha! Or, as good Welsh poet Henry Vaughan had it, *I live again in dying, / And rich am I, now, amid ruins lying.*

I was an infant, mewling with the lady I loved best: Rachel Cariad, my godmother. She went, all puffed up from illness, playing the piano (true story) and at her funeral, her husband threw in a picture of their nasty dog with scoops of earth and wedding ring. My mother, the late sainted woman, scowling now (watch out, sinners!), said, 'He can be married to his mammy now,' and husband scuttled off with Mammy and ignored the other mourners, and that was how it went. But I loved her, see? Rachel Cariad. He was a monster, kept chinchillas, furry little bastards, out back, and he was a tower of wobbling flesh, coddled by Mammy at forty-five, and on burial day, it was time for spotted dick, Friday pudding, so home he went as Rachel Cariad lay in her pit, and I wept and thought, 'Yesterday, I was a child, but today I am fully grown and I am fourteen and whatever happens now, I will never have to marry him and I will get away from my own mammy and I will do it for Rachel Cariad who was beautiful, divinely clever and all snuffed out young. And it wasn't fair, and where were you, Oh God, or you, Duw, I was praying to you by your cathedral, but what were you doing, you *sudd drwg*?' And that means something like naughty fucker in the salt tongue, and I cannot apologise for blasphemy because Jesus likes the ones with spirit who tangle and rage and mean it. And I knew then I would always work with the dead ones, whether the cutting, excising, digging, burying, or putting back together like a carmine jigsaw, is it.

Even though, I tell you, Mr God and I, well, we don't always get on.

It is because of his temper, the naughty fucker, though I love him and would do anything for him and Jesus, *bach*. But it was not enough, the rage, to stop him in his tracks, my Mr God. There were Grandma and Grandma again; one toes up in damp quiet hospital, Bristol way. Bristol granny was full of spite, and when I was a tiny thing, she terrified me with winding sheets of tripe. In her unloving house ere pickled eggs and nasty, wrinkling corpse-toe pickled onions, and I felt, as a child, my childhood left at door, and I had to be big and not scared. She burned things she didn't like: books, pictures, harridans from the village. At school, the grandmas were kindly old things, with sweets and soft stuff. Not in my line. Those were big and hard-knuckled, but at least they taught me how to wrestle, good and hard. I won pounds with the lads, though I never got off with them, like my pretty delicate friends with their weird, alive families. I was lost; I felt it like grief, you see. But, my God, now I see what it gifted me. The loss. I could stand staring into the future, and there was nothing you could do to frighten me. Not a thing.

And second Grandma, whizz-pop in bed. I'd hoped she'd die seeing visions of the Virgin Mary, little white lady in the corner of a Pembrokeshire room, like my nanny did, but she just slipped back and sighed, off Cardiff Bay, so to speak, and it was a bit sad and lacked colour. And afterwards, I went down Penarth beach, wading too deeply into the mud and roaring so the kids said, 'Look, there's that weird,' and I said, to the wind off the sea, 'But I'm not scared. There is nothing you can take. I'm as old as the hills now I'm fifteen.'

I forgot Grandpa, under the damson tree, bottom of the ladder. Died doing what he loved, isn't it? Well, no, he died falling from a ladder, and I would not choose that, boyo, and I doubt many have it in mind. I raged again, and Mr God he said, I heard him in a shoo-in off Cardigan Bay with the devil, he said, 'There's Dafyddnow' – which was me – 'and I'm proud of him, isn't it, with that blasphemy and all because I like the ones who tangle and rage,' and we all know God is Welsh, of course. In the tongue, *Ach, Yr ydym i gyd yn gwybod mai Duw yw Cymraeg!* God, those gorgeous words in my mouth like sweet stuff and best rum!

Ah. Excusing me for a minute because there came a mourner, and I had to doff my hat.

You might think I was finished, but no. I had been raised on terrible deaths on both sides. I could tell you about some of the ones I have buried, too, my God and the kid Jesus and a lamb! Falls from horses; at least two who never got out of bed, and I heard whispering of overwork because they didn't want to say insane, and one disappeared, but I'm sure I saw shuffling out back; then another grandpa sloughed off quietly, quietly; oh and Daddy in my arms and that was the worst because he was spitting curses and saying, 'Not you, not you. Why are you here?' and I eighteen then, but old enough to be my own mother, and Mammy in hospital and keening, 'Where's my boy, my special boy?' when I rocked up at twenty, undergraduate and all, then I prayed by her grave and thought, 'Oh why, she wouldn't want me here,' and that was that. Give me my word-hoard. *Chasm. Sepulchre. Bag of liquorice to condole in an aniseed way.*

Sometimes, at work, if it is someone I know, I chuck in a bag of specials once the family's gone and I am getting the earth done, like. Sweeties. Not for the condoling, but a snack. I do not know how long it is between burial and heaven, see. Or if there is a bit where you come back alive, and you are bloody hungry with the waiting you did. Do not laugh at me, because do you know the answer, do you? Do you now? Well, I am thinking not, *Duw da!*

Off the headland, St David's way, there's a field, bloody big, that's all our own, and it's stuffed with my Llewellyns, poker straight and missing coracle shells, while the primroses push up around them and, time up, the blackberries come up all about, and that it's the time for my aunt Muffled Myfanwy to visit her shot son, for his birthday. Her word-hoard is in her head, and she says, 'My darling, my baby, why no. In carmine and ermine and beautiful days in the sod, my cliff child,' – or something. I startled you? I knew it. I grew up in the strangeness and in the death. But it was not meant, my startling. I swear it is the Cymraeg in me, or something. What I write about, I suppose I always knew, well it is plangent, cruel dysfunction, is it not?

Ha! No, of course it is not. It is survival and hoisting above your head this beautiful word-hoard, like your standard and going, 'Raaar!' Merrily in two languages or more, with midnight blue and gunmetal garlands in the dark. I learned to give sorrow words. You can take those words, my cariads, across the Atlantic – I should like to think my words touch the American folk because I always felt the English lack sensitivity and a good ear – and not only words but colour. Or imaginary friends. Literary creations. Say, the Dead Dears of Dylan Thomas, though I am big on the Southern gothic because they could be Welsh, see; they have got the natural gruesome, all done up poetic. Where was I? Ah, the literaries. We had many chats when I was growing up. And then me and Dead Dylan. Went to his writing shed in Laugharne and communed with him. Smoked a bit. Where was I again? My nanny on the Cleddau, my great grandmother who smoked a pipe, spat, and terrified the gentry, saw a little white woman in the corner for years and prayed with great aplomb to the Virgin Mary, and death was actually scared of her. Everyone and everything were scared of feared Nanny. She taught me to see things. When she died, it was a scarring pain, but it was triumphant, and that was a fine thing. Though I am not saying it can always be so.

I do say that people lie about what scares them.

I think that is why some people do the running thing in the odd kit and the bouncing shoes. That if they run hard enough, they will outwit death. But then. My great Uncle Harry was the best wrestler this side of Tregarron; hard as nails, irresistible to women; oiled his chest just so. There were those who thought our Harry was immortal. But still, he fell off the platform at Bristol Temple Meads and got crushed between buffers, and it didn't matter then about his washboard or how fast he could get to Llansteffan with the wind against him.

So yes, loss: seen it so many times. It will happen again. In a quiet moment or on a balmy day when you are going to a yellow beach. And I have seen those who did not care buff up the plate on a coffin and watched those who hoped for cash hoist a coffin. Funerals are useful in that way, for me: a sorting device. You can tell a lot about a man by the way he behaves around an open casket. In my head, there are people I have banned from my own service already. But if I cannot control that, they are at least off my Christmas card list: that is a few seconds gained when I can instead write a card to crying eyes down the road who watches and wants company and love. There is a moment gained to help undo a folded lie, and I can stand here, in the quiet hole, and watch a field vole caper, the incursion of rat or worm. Set a shield bug on my hand, and all is calm. You could, too. Now the reaper's set you straight, that is. Yes, look: the bad man who corpse gloats and thinks he impresses; the cad who prays big and only in public, *whose* eyes are kind at the wake and whose flowers are devotion, not show? You go and think you are mired in loss, in a terrible deficit. Of course, but there is benefit to accrue to you if only you are attentive. Scythe.

Do some losing.

That title, at top. It is from Macbeth, bard boy. It runs, 'Give sorrow words; the grief that does not speak knits up the o'er wrought heart and bids it break.' I am handy with a spade and digging in the dead. It's my job, and I'd not have it any other way, but I say to you this: name, shape, hue. Care for your own heart and devise a vocabulary for your loss, unique to you. It comes to us all, but with a word-hoard, you will not be alone. Remember too, that in darkness, as I have seen, there are navy and lavender lights and a star which laughs. And know that I, your humble gravedigger, will inter you with love and chuck in some sherbet lemons or taffy for your journey, like.

An Angry Starlet Retires
to the Shenandoah

You see my pure acetylene glow there? In the picture you found on the table and could not remember placing there for you had certainly thrown it out? Yes. Oh yes. That one.

Hello, sweet one. Hello again. I am smooth, and rather than blinking like a mewling baby into a first light, I face it confidently. Look at my face. It is hard to avert a gaze, I expect, because of the softness of skin, unfurrowed by care. You want to run your finger across my cheek, don't you, sweet darling? A pelt like alabaster. But I would not advise a touch. Or my hair; it has thinned a bit, and do you know how long it takes me and those I employ to truss it up and scaffold it, huh? I have closed my eyes as is traditional. I do not care for the trend of having the photograph retouched and your open eyes inked in.

You, open eyes. Where is your scaffold? You cannot climb out, can you? You can't escape now from where I've put you. Neither can she. Nor reach for you. Well, you should have appreciated my star quality, baby. But I tell you, moving from Atlanta to this place, all proper, well, I want to create hell. I deserve it. The people are so smug, and there is not a hint of proper glamour or sex. No one has ever had sex in this place, Bellend, Virginia. I know all about places like this, so I thought I'd come here to fix a mess and cast some spite. They hate people from out of town. I've seen a sticker some of them have: it says, 'We don't care how you did it THERE', and I think, 'You will, bitches.' I deserve to create merry hell in someone's gloating decorum.

But let's talk about me. And you. With a swipe at *her*. Days before, I had been banging pots and looking at grey hairs. 'Christmas shopping,' you said. 'Oh yes,' I thought, 'Oh yes, I can tolerate this because I'll be bought something beautiful, and he's so handsome. Everyone says so.' But really, as I fought sleet and myriad people, never basking in those festive sounds or scenting with happiness the smell of mulled wine – you remember? In the Abbey Square against the sparkles of advent as the choirboys sang – well, I knew. Saw myself for what I was. Correction: saw myself through your eyes. I was, as I'd heard you say before of women, losing it. Whereas before, you longed for me, breasts high, all the things you commended me for. Such integument (not that you had known this word) and the sashay I had, watching me from behind. All those enticements. When we met.

How things change.

I became a nag. That sex. It dried up, and what was I? She who did and cared and bought and fought. Whose sashay had departed for shuffle; whose integument was hard old whore-hide. Who watched, in a tired old cliché, the opportunities desiccate. Became invisible. Well, how dare you? I was a sensation on the stage, starlet and illumined. I do not do dishes.

You stopped seeing me, and how could you, someone like me?

Ah, but there's more than one side to not being seen. When you are invisible, your spectation is better. And while you lured and played and thought, 'Ah well, still carping on, but she'll never know!' and your pretty little trinket girl clinked on your arm and looked like tinsel, well now, as I said, you did not see me as I was. I've history, you know. I change if I must. My pockets and the books you laughed at – yes; Tinsel laughed and fucked; she did not read: there's sneering but hoo, boy – those things are full of spells and hexes and words so beautiful they'll eat you up. Which, as you gather, they did. Somewhere in the background, in the lilac room behind the pure acetylene woman whose skin you long to touch, there's you. I wove you into the heart of a star. A fine amaranthine one, and she is in there with you – but I'm not a savage. Look how gorgeous your confinement is!

I regret nothing. I do not regret what I haven't done yet and, baby, the sweet chaos Momma's going to cause.

Let me put a picture closer to your eyes? See.

Oh, clever boy, it is not the one from the table you thought you had thrown out. Why no, sweet dear. It's another, blown in like an acer leaf in breeze; calmed in like a dainty bird on a waft of the embalmer's sap gone to ether. Post-mortem and pretty.

And there I am. I have emerged, growing, hungry, for the new year, the chrysalid you never expected. A spell for you, then a present for myself. Haven't decided on the hair yet, but, my God, can you see my eyelashes and silver eyes? Should I say, imagine them because, to you, my eyes look closed. But I see as I saw then, when my heart stopped as you both set my anger sweltering.

I want to swoon when I see my reflection. Never going to be old. We will just scaffold, frame, adjust the lighting. Sit me better upright with some sort of frame, perhaps? It has no end, really. I am dead already, but it's just beginning, boy. This new play.

Not Waving, but Drowning*

Abraham Jones lived a simple kind of life: pleasant place to live, nice wife – nothing spectacular but homely and something to be thankful for: both the home and the wife. Went to work, did well: again, nothing spectacular, but reliable. *Good old Jones,* they said – and always thanked him heartily at the staff Christmas party before laughing behind his back about his boring wife and his poor jokes and what a sucky, sucky, sucker he was. He never quite got promoted. Kids came along; usual ups and downs; things went, he thought, tolerably well, and he loved his girls, though sometimes he might have wished for boys. Holidays in a nice spot; savings and annuities; mortgage paid up well in advance of retirement because of his diligence.

Diligence tries to scream, you know. But it cannot get it out: because it is diligent, alright? And all the time, he smiled. At the neighbours; at the tetchy mother-in-law; waved his daughters off to new homes and college and husbands; he wanted to please and had been brought up so to do. And exhaustively so. But inside? Well, he ground his teeth and said ineffective hexes and wished bad things and then took them back because

---

*Inspired by 'Not Waving but Drowning' by Stevie Smith.

he was good, good, good, yet he could scream with the boredom and the Mr Nicey. Nobody is so uncomplicated. Every now and then, he would have an unsettling feeling, a catching in the throat, sort of strange cascading feeling inside. Then a tightness in the throat. Grinding teeth again. He wanted to call to someone that it was an emergency – but of what kind? No one was hurt, all was well, and if he were the man swimming way out at sea, you might look at him from your place on the beach and think he was larking about, waving at you, inviting you to come out, too.

Yes, come out, come, Abraham Jones! The water's lovely. But the truth was, he was drowning. And always had been. And nobody knew it. 'I wish,' he said, 'That I'd never taken back the hexes. I wish I weren't Abraham Jones.'

Out he went during some sensible beaching. Wife and big kids now on the Soleros and sun slap. Out and out. You could barely see him. Too far. *I will give them a scare* came an impulse. It thrilled him. So Abraham bobbed down below the water until he was dizzy, then bobbed up and waved. No reaction. They had not even noticed. He did it again and again. Same non-reaction, *oh God*. It didn't even matter if he were waving or drowning. But now came a slap against him, something wielding its cumbersome body up and down, up and down. A sunfish. Slap and bob. Him and the fish. It hadn't meant to hurt him, but he was weakened and drifted on a wave closer to shore. Then they saw him, and, by obligation, strong swimmers brought him in as his wife wailed, and the kids found sand gapers and augers to finesse the castle. He lay on the beach, dead and grinning.

Now, his wife eyed a tardy lifeguard.

Poor Old Croft*

Poor old Croft. The fool on the hill: laughed at as a child by the other boys because not only was he slow at his work, but he had two left feet for the football. Still, though, his mother shed a tear for him, and Croft plugged on. This boy was gauche socially, never made it with the girls when he was a teenager, but he was brave enough to ask them out anyway. Even if the less sweet ones snickered while he blushed and wished he could run away. And again, his mother, a dark horse true enough, shed a tear for him; his father said nothing and carried on with his woodworking, and Croft, all fingers and thumbs, tried to help him.

Poor old Croft.

Sometimes he wanted to shed a tear, too. But he just plugged away, getting the measurements wrong and getting in the way. And then, eventually, he was all grown up and sitting up there in the loft of the barn. He loved his animals and would coo and fawn to them. He loved them, and they would cluster around him for a boy needs company, whether terrestrial, of the aether or *Athene noctua*, like you would see in the

---

*Inspired by 'Croft' by Stevie Smith.

pictures his sweet mother took on a day when Croft wore his best and flattest shirt. A boy's best friend can be an owl.

Ah, but reader, that is not where it ends. Did you think that he had nothing but lazy feet and a fuzzy head? It's all in the plugging away and the kind tear of a devoted mother. And that miscreant hardening-off such as happens to kindness if it's mocked and mocked. Oh, and spells. It helps if your mother is conversant with the grimoire because, even if she can't fix you up, she'll fix up the others who hurt you. Because that's how mothers are, alive or dead. My goodness, how it hurt her to see him fail in the eyes of others.

But now, picture him sitting up there in the loft with his best and flattened hair and *Athene noctua*. Croft built that barn, you see; got there in the end. And it was beautiful and even more so for its integral flaws, so hard to avoid for soft and square-thumbed Croft. And it lasted and lasted. The barn is still there with the kind spells and warmth of a doting mother. She buried the bad boys or scared them out of town in a yellow sort of way they could not explain. Like smoke in a dream and a big old skull gnashing mandible, so weird you could not say. They'd put you in the asylum. And Croft is not really the silly boy-man to be laughed at. Remember that the fool on the hill might be the one who sees the world in its clearest, most luminous state and that, one day, he might get the girl, too. Tenderly, in the soft hay of the loft. All those other boys fell off the ladder because witch-mother pulled the rungs off in a spell as they climbed up to taunt him or get the girl. Good boy. Good Croft. Soft. Good for you. And *Athene noctua* laughs for you and loves you, alive or dead.

The Peel

'My life and world are frowsty. I think that I am, too. And WHAT IS MORE WHAT DO YOU HAVE TO DO TO GET A MAN ROUND HERE?'

And with that, Adeline began researching what to do; a whole new you, sloughed off and revealed. New friends, clothes, and ideas. But why not start with the face, though not before research?

Chemical peels are liquids brushed onto the face to remove dead skin cells and stimulate the growth of new cells. The aim of this cosmetic procedure is to improve the appearance of the facial skin, expunging or at least reducing caramel age spots and evening out skin tone. Going for a Kardashian. Or something. It must all be possible. Adeline discovered that there were three types of peel: superficial, medium, and deep, with superficial and medium peels usually being safe, provided they're administered correctly, and deeper peels constituting more of a risk. The first two were entirely temporal, fleeting, in their impact; the third, long-lasting, though expensive, painful, and, as I said, risky. Yet, this third peel was immediately attractive to her, for surely working on a deeper level was appropriate for one to banish such a degree of frowstiness. She booked in, prepared for sedation and a period of exclusion afterwards, for redness and snake scales and moth wings of whatever layers of old Adeline looked like. And she would be beautiful, then. And happy. And even though it was hard to get a man around here, they present if your allure is on, and you are buffed up. Fact.

Later, cowering in the chair after an initial blast of confidence, Adeline was prepped and masked and exfoliated and, duly, peeled. She was prepared for the red and the moth wings and snake scales that would fall, but not that they would keep on falling.

The following day, waking as if in a nest of soap flakes, a shiver. She did not feel quite herself. The day after that, walking home from an outing she had enforced on herself but followed by a skin snowstorm, she knew herself to be thinner and smaller; she was less of herself. Looking in the mirror, it was a smaller, thinner Adeline, while the world in her background looked saporous, voluptuous, and old. It was more beautiful, more delicious – and there was a shock. *Why oh why?*

There is a canard truth out there and, if you can, don't let it in. It's a thing you're fed, my darlings, and it's about the joy of having a luminous surface, about polish, about matching your smalls for erotic piquancy, never getting old and what you need for sex, indulgence and joy. Now, I am Adeline's big sister on the other side of that mirror, and I feel sorry about the sloughing off and the moth wings and snakeskin; it's unnecessary. Oh, and I will get you, though I do not try to be cruel. I do not take; I just get given. And, oddly enough, I am eternal and have never not been here and can never not exist. So, I will tell you truths that are not canard, but echt-truth and pure.

No one *really* needs a polish because intellect doesn't buff, and intellect is sex, appetite and interest. And passion, that's good, too. No one who gets you within twenty metres of the bedroom door (I say that as an approximation) cares if your smalls don't match because you're already there, and if they do, *sling*. Life is remarkably short. Age is going to visit, but that's when you take the intellect and brine it, so you light it. That's when you dare, and you say, OH YES, I WILL and not, OH NO, I DARE NOT. And if you are bed-bound or crutched, then burn and think it. All those people and now poor Adeline. There is no hierarchy; in the end, my worms will get you, or you burn, so while you stamp on earth, your only peel, your only deep peel, should be the insatiable scouring of oranges in a bed with your lover. Or the mango in the bath. Or what you reveal of yourself because you are who you are, and that is fine. Oh yes.

Hmm, baby, hmm. Said Adeline, 'My life and world are frowsty. I think that I am, too. And WHAT IS MORE WHAT DO YOU HAVE TO DO TO GET A MAN ROUND HERE?' So, don't worry about the peel and cowering in the chair; remember the mismatched and boldly worn smalls, the oranges and the mangoes in the bath. And the worm food. And you, my sweet ones, will be fine, and I should know.

When I Was, That Was I

If you were to stroll out on the headland beyond the cathedral city and towards the place where the land rounds big in one place and dips down in a crevice field in the other, and at any time of day, you would have met the Virgin Mary. And my God and the Baby Jesus, what a view Our Lady had out over the sea.

Mary lived in a pretty shrine: a tall arch. She wore the usual and was ever so lovely, I always thought; there were little jars of flowers by her dainty feet; one hand was over her heart, and the other extended to you, headland tramper and pilgrim. And surely, I cannot have been the *only* one to notice that her hands were not always in this position. Sometimes, she had her hands like this, see, in my picture. It was a welcome picture but a sad one, and sometimes when I caught her eye and regarded the tilt of the head – which looked slightly melancholy to me – I thought those outstretched hands connoted exasperation. And that might have come from listening to prayers, receiving blossoms, or descrying long-stifled tears in the headland trampers. Or maybe all the pressure from being Mother of God, or possibly the glare in her eyes from the Wilkinson's solar garden lights the local nuns had put in the arch by her feet.

If you had looked below Mary, following the emerald line towards the cliff where the freshwater ran, you'd have seen the little well. There were coins in there, a coin for a sad thought, maybe, and a prayer; little medallions and tokens and the bubble of sweet water that had caressed the heather and gorse on its way. Pilgrim shinies for a *Speak to the Lord Jesus for Me*. I could understand all of it and could also understand why Mary shifted in her arch. I thought about it when I was out there at night, emerald grass dappled by the Wilkinson's solar lights and the sound of the sea beyond. Oh, what a responsibility to be the vessel of such hope and to be Mother eternal. Can you imagine the crick in the neck and the exhaustion as, all over the world, another Mary and another Mary listened in to the deathly pale and the lonely? To the loss and to those who wanted gain and hegemony – and I'd not have thought less of her if she'd taken a solar light or a little pebble to those last askers because that's not what prayer is for.

Anyway, I was a lonely boy. Born drenched in death and always solitary, oddball. But out there, tramping to Mary, I would wonder what pose her hands would be in. If I'd been beaten, she'd be there, arms outstretched for oddball boy; once, memorable time, I imagined she had the sleeves of her gown rolled up, and her fists clenched like she was going to get them. Mammy, Daddy, the proper boys in school and the snoot girls and Mrs Jenkins at the shop that said I was not a proper boy with my ways that weren't fighting but running away. But our Lady was alright with me.

Because when I tramped on the clifftop and went to see her, that was when I knew that, when I was, then was I. My stretched idiom was no stretch for the Virgin Mary, and she knew that I meant, in my thoughts, that when I was there, I was me and at ease. I lounged into the darkness of azure nights and said my prayers and I made it through to others like me. Then I was less alone. And when my death came, as it did too soon and salty, you might say, there she was, elegant marble before fleshly Mother and, either way, she was miracle.

Dead Etiquette

There was much to think about, I discovered, dear death-in-life reader, when starting out in my delicate business venture.

Mortuary practice and all the accoutrements of the beyond need tender body and careful thoughts. You cannot be heavy-handed, although, as you shall see, the problem was not my hands but my poor heart, and I hope I do not express any of this badly.

I got advice from Evans the Bodies (you remember him from earlier in this, your own book?) and oh how I missed him because even now I was in England, up the blasted sinews of the motorway, for when I was at home, I was in a better place, but travellers and undertakers must be content. And that, if you're church-going, is a saying from The Old Testament, which is repeated by Peredur in *The M**abinogi*. Now, I would cry for the homesickness when I telephoned Evans the Bodies, but he boomed and told me things to think of and how to build. He said to think of this, and of that, now: of God I yearned, oh *hiraeth*, to hear his voice rattle and boom down the line, like the choir in church ringing on the very earth under the flagstones.

'Boy, you must think of the location of a funeral home be-cause it needs to be well for those who want to see the Dead Dears. First, you will need enough space for visitations, and you must have office space because, remember now, Almost, the records are all important, is it. I have made some dreadful mistakes in my time. Jenkins of Nevern has for years been vis-iting his wife in the wrong place, but you won't tell, I am sure. Now, boy, you will also need an area separate from the main showing area for embalming and cremation. Like our tables for Myfanwy and me, see? You cannot be draining near the showing, and we can't have trimming-up and puffing-round or buckets and tubes near the visited departments, although I've had a few spiteful relatives ask in my time. Remember me telling you about Timothy the Nasty of Little Haven? Asked to see his wife while we were preparing to check that she was re-ally gone. 'Timothy,' I said, 'I know you are grieving, but that is not a thing you should do. It is not respectful.'

'She was a thing of darkness,' said he, 'And I need to tell Her at The Sloop while the bed is unmade.'

That was his mistress, of course, and now I say that to you again, I do see that circumstances and speech were a little sus-picious – but we move on, boy, we move on. And as I was say-ing, finally, you two boys will need an area where coffins and clothes and the other bits and pieces involved in planning and decorating the funeral can be set up for display, see. Now that is something I always wanted at my place. Myfanwy (once my love could speak) told me quite firmly that we didn't need it, but I had always wanted a sort of gallery or a shop; lovely things for sad times where you could choose your shade of crêpe, but Myfanwy, she said, 'No that is morbid and a shade too far, Evans the Bodies' although she does let me have my velvet corner where I keep the Dead Dears' possessions: all the surprising books of beauty from the folk we think, in life, do not read. But we are wrong, Almost, wrong. We do not see inside their souls, and you do not know the intellect of another if he will not speak. Now, finally, pay attention to parking space, but I am bound to say that you should not charge for parking. You remember the protests over that in Pembroke? And then you need think of how you will be moving the Dead Dears from your premises to the street for funeral processions.'

'So much, then, to think about!'

'Well, I have more to say!' Evans the Bodies was declaiming again in his catalogue voice, that which had won Myfanwy, with my help, of course. The morbid but discerning woman likes this voice, Evans had once told me: it showed you were enthusiastic, good of remembrance and in command.

'Now, the equipment you will need to run a proper job with the Dead Dears is going to cost thousands, Almost. You remember me talking to you about this all? Keep a Ledger of Death, both. Now when I bought my embalming kit, it came from that sour fellow in Carmarthen, and it cost three thousand pounds. Do not go cheap, though. A good finish and a proper craftsmen's make are a proper send-off, however bitten the corpse. Then, you will be needing your embalming table, and you mustn't skimp on build quality. That I learned to very poor disadvantage because when I was doing up Timothy the Nasty's wife, there was a merry tumble as he came in to gloat, see? So, build quality is all, boy. You will need your refrigerated storage, and really, I should say hydraulic lifts, but then I finds Myfanwy and I can do most of that. I am a strong man for hefting and cradling my Dead Dears. Have you thought out the rest? Are you thinking of offering cremation services, for then you'll need a cremation system as well, but we will talk more about this because it isn't my favoured way to go and, round here, we have plenty of turf, see? Places from away? Well, I expect that they are that crowded, so look into it all? Or go unofficial and see if they can quietly push them up a bit for room, like, in the burial ground. You could consider the memory tubes I used to talk about. They will be in the catalogues. Make sure who's who. Now your products: you should know all this, but caskets, clothing, embalming fluid, hairdressing and make-up, and urns if you are providing cremation services. Oh, there are beauties in my catalogues, as I have told, and don't forget the full or the partial: is the Dead Dear to be seen or obscured? With the memory tubes and all, little pieces of delicacy, boy. Now, the cost of these items can vary, and you must be calm but hard-headed: you must negotiate the best price possible, and that isn't wrong though you're not on the market bargaining for fish. And you have to think of your furnishing: I am told there is a thing called shabby chic, but that is not it at all for your proper work. You want plain, tidy chairs to keep grieving loved ones comfortable and content those who are pretending to grieve or even slightly pleased. A small table is good in case tea is required, but I should add that, in our business, it is vital, Almost, vital, to keep urns and receptacles separate and apart, or all Hell will break loose if you make tea with the wrong thing. If you are having hot drinks, then in my view, coasters are also important because mug rings on a table in a funeral parlour are what Myfanwy once called *infra dig*, which, boy, is the Greek tongue. She is a clever lady and the light of my life. As I was saying, I heard tell that some people (and I expect mostly abroad folk) have sofas and even a small snack room, but that seems to me a shade too, what is it, *decorous* for the occasion. 'Cake is for the wake.' Myfanwy, is that what you said, my love? And you're not wanting the parlour to look like a Little Chef.'

Came a voice: 'Yes, Evans. Tea and remember the sugar and milk, but small biscuits on a nice plate is not going too far. With doilies for a nice touch.'

'Now, have you thought about the hearse and the lead car? That'll be tens of thousands of pounds, boy. But you can lease. I will see what I can find out for up your way. And bargain, boy, bargain. There is no shame, but you do not do it like you are common. And get a discount on the insurance. Tell the business fellows you'll provide for them in their demise, tidy-like. And there's general liability insurance. You remember all this from college, yes? Two kinds, write them down and bargain like a professional, boy. Two kinds of insurance, yes? And don't confuse them. Not as though you can insure against death, is it? Even with the faith. Myfanwy's husband and brother and so all praying to the Virgin and your sister Perfection, too, and that was not insurance, now was it, lad?' And there came a sweet woman's voice that was rather more booming than muffled:

'Evans the Bodies! That is irreligious and no way to be speaking, even though you are my true love.'

Slowly slowly, we put the business together, Ned, my business partner and I, though the demands of the locals were harsh. They wanted green burials, and we could not cater. Cardboard coffins which embarrassed me. Would not stand for anything other than natural materials in the caskets, while we loved the crackle of polyester as I had had with Evans. And some of them thought we were common, I expect, but we did our best. Halls decked out like the Taj Mahal; churches without proper singing: I mean without the boom and clarion call of the Welsh voice. There was a reverberation missing in the polite singing, and I realised I was homesick to the core and heartsick for Seren, who, though sour, was the most beautiful thing in the world to me. We laboured on, though. We had premises, all proper, and everything as Evans the Bodies had recommended.

But all this time, I was emptier than the waiting coffins. And here was why.

I had been mired in death, then trained in it. I was not afraid, and I was good at it and knew that death and its precincts instruct us just as much as life. And when, as I worked and learned to get better at our trade from Evans the Bodies, I saw losses and some which might have been interrupted or stopped; and when I saw bodies vital and faces still so full of brooding and intellectual rapacity; of possibility – oh then I would ponder that life may be brief, but death is long. And so, you want a bit of thought for the latter, and I have come to the conclusion that a lust for life, or truly an insensate passion, is what you'll be wanting for the former. And there we are, see.

I was spending all my days with the Dead Dears, but life was cold. And the truth was that, despite my attentions to the beyond people and quiet conversations with them as I laid them ready, well, I was lonely, and my heart rent.

Love, Now and Then,
on a Primrose Bank

When Emrys died, he'd be insisting, I knew, on a natural burial, and so, when he went, like the good wife, I paid up for The Wonderful Field and did what he would have wanted. Afterwards, we had a grid map of the Field, overlooking the Tawe river, and you could have walked across that field without the slightest idea of the folk underfoot. No stones, no markings; just an incongruous B&Q arbour that someone had put up in the corner of the Field, replete with pictures of the collie and grandchildren plus the best kit car that Beloved had ever assembled. A picture of it, not the car, because that would have been truly odd, though arresting. The grid map: so those that wanted could visit the right person, there being no stones or markings. Emrys had once said he'd fancied an elaborate rockery so as not to be outdone by the B&Q arbour, but I felt I had brooked enough and declined to carry out the wish. Then I was not the good wife.

Emrys had lots of friends. I knew them all from nights in The Cambrian. I mean, I knew them as they were in that setting. Knew how he was there, warm to others. When he died, they trooped to The Wonderful Field, and we had poems and songs, then drinks and a good tea back at The Cambrian.

I had loved Emrys in a concave sort of way, a trying way. Oh! I had never felt what I had dreamed of: the idea of being with a reverent man on a primrose bank. Feeling the half-hot and beguiling breath of spring on our stomachs and breathing in the picante scent of the primroses warmed on the bank. Feeling the pull of knowing that you are wanted, crows' feet and half-baked idea; new again in love and basking in bed. Desired and, I will not say worshipped, but still, I had a bold fantasy of a man falling to his knees in front of me, burying his face in my stomach, making a kind of sigh, or an *ach ach* sound, then rising and carrying me to bed.

I got, *I suppose we should get married* and a cold rutting in the dark. And Emrys wasn't cruel, but I tell you he turned out to be arctic and our bed, our home, were desolate. There was no one I could tell, though I am setting it down now.

To the outside world, he was a big man, my Emrys. Strong and desirable; desiring. But no, he was ice, and it was only I who knew.

All this I was thinking in The Wonderful Field and at the tea party. Llinos of The Cambrian had done it all up posh, with cakes and rolled sandwiches, and there were crabsticks and vol au vents, and he would have loved it all because he liked this kind of feast. But that was the thing. I'd thought it would change if I had tried the feasting at home. If I were a hot Lampeter Mrs Waters the whore to his Ammanford Tom Jones; a hungry strumpet, a tearer of flesh. And I'd tried this sort of feast and tried to look flustered and angry while eating like a man, but no: no matter what I did, he never ate with gusto, just silence, flicking on his phone, the paper. Sighing. None of the *ach ach* and the kneeling and the carrying off. So, it was more like I was old Siân with the cataracts who makes jam for the Women's Institute in Llandeilo.

Poor Emrys, though. A runaway tractor from Douglas's top field while Emrys was out mending the fence at the bottom of our fields. It was quick; he had his music in and did not hear it. He was listening to what roused him most: old Tom Jones, and I expect it was 'Delilah' and he was mouthing it hot. And when I say Tom Jones, I mean Tom Jones from Pontypridd the singer, not Tom Jones in the book whose Mrs Waters I had tried to be.

It comes to us all, death, that kind of ravishment, and for some of us when we are listening to Tom Jones. With Mammy, it was while she was baking bara brith when she had *Antiques Roadshow* on, criticising Fiona Bruce's knowing and arched eyebrows; down, mid-sentence and Fiona clickbaiting for a car boot Fabergé egg, *Good God*. With Daddy, well he was playing his cornet during the eisteddfod and down he went. It took a while to extract him because the others were too stubborn to stop playing, and his nasty band didn't like him anyway. But I was telling you about my Emrys. Another sudden one, it was.

Ah yes. Even in the midst of life, we are in death. Yes, in the Welsh tongue, *yng nghanol bywyd rydym yn marw*, as it says in *The Mabinogi* and, I think, in that Tom Jones song about the green grass. Now, there is more to this story, and there are people around here who won't talk to me now. You see, I knew everyone at his funeral, snaking down the Towy valley, but one. She was a pretty thing, a refined sort of woman, and I remember that she had the palest of lilac gloves on and good shoes and hat. She was gorgeous, hatefully so. I don't give that sort of compliment lightly. And I could feel her pulsing, that one. And then suddenly she caught my eye, and I knew just so that Emrys was only cold with *me*; that I was keeper and baker and that this was the woman for whom he had fallen to his knees, pressed his head on her stomach like he'd worshipped her, and then carried her off to a hot bed, somewhere, going *ach ach*, or I don't know. And then I knew cold fury. I knew this was not a woman who scraped carrots or bought him Tom Jones posters or helped him to castrate the cattle. No, here was beauty and class and hands that were soft under those lilac gloves.

I buried it in myself, this knowing, during the vol au vents and the crabsticks and the condoling at The Cambrian, after, like. And I buried it in myself all night and was a good and dignified widow: I buried my blind fury and my generous compliments for her and tried to sleep, but then began to spit ire, and so I sat up until dawn and, possessed with more cold fury than I ever felt before. Hot-vexed with memories of my arctic life, I think I went mad, though I was righteous because I went out with a spade and determined to dig him up.

I'd a few questions to ask and a few things to say.

I'd mislaid the grid map but thought I knew where he was in The Wonderful Field, and so I dug. Down *down*. Struck right, I thought. But it wasn't him. Just some rubble and shreds of old farmers' sacks; then again, nearby, I hit glass of an old Victorian bottle dump. Then again and again, ach but now: instead – I could tell by the remains of her handbag with its gold clasp – I hit Mrs Jones of the big house and had to stuff her back in, say sorry. Then again, Dewi and his brother Alun who'd died in a bizarre duel of some sort and were popped in together. I did a prayer and a *hello boys* and went on digging. Well, I could not find the bastard, and by the time I did, I'd furrowed a mighty section of that bloody field so that, when the constabulary and a few from the village had arrived, The Wonderful Field had been ploughed. But by that time, I'd said all the terrible things I'd needed to mouth at Emrys and questioned him about my cold rogering, and I swear – I swear it now – he'd laughed at me and told me of the sweltering bed with his mistress. So sweltering they didn't even have a duvet. He'd been there, Tom Jones with his real Mrs Waters, the lilac-gloved doxy, when I thought he was at the cattle auction in Carmarthen. So much for her refinement, then! Like beasts and only with sheets, my God. No duvet, and I bet in the light, too.

I still feel, I must say, that those in the village and in the constabulary were unsympathetic to me. So too, the staff at the place with the barbed wire on the coast road out of Haverfordwest, and it's not fair.

But I'll tell you this. I'm out now, and it isn't me who's styed in The Wonderful Field, and I've mattress money to spend because I wasn't all daft for that iceberg man. The Wonderful Field is tidy, for they've rollered and returfed the righteous damage I caused it. And it's said that the lady with the pale lilac gloves goes to visit, and I am biding my time. My spade is too good to swing at her, but I will go and have a sultry life before long, and *I will too*, and I will throw a curse up at The Wonderful Field and follow the snaking Towy to a new life. Finding a complicit soul and on a spring day, feeling the half-hot and beguiling breath of the season on our stomachs and suspiring the picante scent of the primroses warmed on the bank. And that is what we will do until the day we are ravished too.

That is my plan, Arctic Emrys and your lost, lilac-gloved lover.

The Mirror

Poor Rhea. Imagine her in front of a tall mirror, hair to her knees and its lengths crimped like you had smoothed her with your muffin cutter. She was a lovely girl who had fallen on hard times. She had lots of sisters and, of all of them, she was quite the jolliest. She told great stories. She was funny and vivacious, and her laugh was contagious. Unfortunately, though, the mistress in whose service she lived was very cross with her. With her chatter, her jokes, and her cheerful temperament, she had been deliberately employed to distract her mistress from the fact that her husband, shall we say, played away. Or sometimes just to distract her mistress from jealous musings and hot temper. When, one day, the mistress found out she had been duped, the mistress looked for revenge – although Rhea was, sadly, only the scapegoat.

I told you that Rhea loved to talk. Well, her punishment from her mistress – who had the devil and sorcery in her when she was in the worst of funks – was that she would be struck dumb. A song, a joke, a story might be forever on her lips, but she could not share. Instead, the most tiresome thing ever: she would simply only be able to repeat the last words she had heard spoken. So, Rhea, while able to use her voice, could only imitate. She left her band of sisters and went, melancholy beyond words, to live all alone. She lived, I think, amongst the trees on the high slopes of the mountain.

One day, though, a fine-looking man was hunting with his friends amongst these trees. He got separated from them and was disoriented and quite, *quite* lost. Rhea saw him and was spellbound: he was the most beautiful man she had ever seen. She was spirited away; time stood still, and nothing else mattered. And for a moment, she even forgot the wicked punishment meted out to her by her nasty former mistress. Ah, but, reader., the fine face can hide a cruel and self-interested interior: where there is little kindness or admiration for the kindness, wit, or imagination of others, only a delight in oneself. Ascanius had grown up pleasing himself, and because he loved only himself, he had never felt what Rhea felt now. So, Ascanius wandered, and Rhea followed him at a distance. Eventually, he began to look a little unsettled: 'Where are you?' he shouted.

Of course, Rhea had no choice but to copy him. He heard her, of course.

'Where are you?' she echoed back. Ooh, you should have seen his face, that pretty boy.

'Answer me!'

And, ooh, the painful irony of this. He could never answer her: never give what she would be able to give. Joy and life and... 'I told you: answer me!'

She could hear the anger in his voice. He accused her to her face of being a temptress and of mocking him. Rhea was in tears. His words came thick and fast, ever more cruel, and Rhea – while she repeated these awful words back, bitter and repugnant to her – lay on the moss and cried.

I hadn't told you how beautiful Rhea was. She would have taken away your breath. I have heard of people like that. Long

long hair with the crinkle, white linens, and lawns that she made look finer than they were. Shiny little shoes, as you see in the picture. I have even wished that one day, I could be like that for someone. Haven't you? Think about this old Urdu poem: 'In love there is no difference between life and death: / We live by gazing on the face that takes away our breath.' Yes, think about that for a while? (And the fact that you learned how mirrors are polyglots.) You would have fallen in love with Rhea, even though you might have found her a chatterbox sometimes. Ascanius, though, did not see her beauty. While she was dumb in her way, in his, he was blind. Because what happened next was this.

Eventually, Ascanius stopped insulting her. Not because he had no more niggard things to say, but because he was worn out. So, he lay down and, yes, his breath was taken. Because he looked into a clear mountain pool as he rested and saw what was for him, the most beautiful face he had ever seen. And he fell immediately and hopelessly in love – not with Rhea, of course, but with the reflection that he had been yet to see: his own. He stretched out his arms to the face in the pool, spoke sweetly and, of course, the handsome reflection whispered back in the voice of Rhea, ending in an, 'I love you.' How those words hurt Rhea. Ascanius tried time and time again to hold the figure in the pool, clasp him and bring him closer. He looked and looked and cried, and the figure cried back, giving back to him what he gave himself. They were now, he thought, inseparable. And in time, Ascanius became desperate and threw himself into the pool to catch his loved one. In the depths, there were only stones and choking weed and darkness and his own death.

So he was gone, and Rhea, bound to him still, could not save him. I heard that she simply wasted away as she longed for him. We can see how futile this was and how unworthy he was, but we don't always make wise choices, we know. We might think with longing for others who can never return our love. Maybe you could go to that mountain and try to talk to Rhea; tell her that you are there and that you understand, maybe? She would answer you back, though, because while her body is gone, she is still doomed to wander and echo back what we say. But you would be company and understanding for her and, maybe, when the light is dappled, and the shadows lengthen, you might just catch the shadow of a beautiful girl...

Nobody ever found the body of our vain and unkind man, who had fallen in love only with himself, but people from this part of the world say that flowers sprang up around the pool where he drowned and where Rhea mourns him – although only in her fleeting and shadowy self – to this day. It is a shame that sometimes love chooses us, and we seem powerless. Most important, though: do not think yourself the centre of the known world but also do not, however swept away, think this of another. I promise you that it will not end well.

Keep this old photograph of her, will you? Let me hand it to you. Look at her just so in the linens she made look fine and the shiny shoes and the long hair with a crinkle? As a memory of her when she was still substantial. Do not worry about Ascanius because, *honestly*.

Terminal Teatime

In a small town in Georgia, the Spanish moss cascades from the live oaks, the red earth is soft and warm, and the benches are white. At this time of year, though, the grass had begun to parch, and, by midday, the frames of the branches were hot to the touch. So, it was good to be in the park with your Kool-Aid, sheltering in what less scorching enclaves you could find and catching the occasional spray from the fountain when a breeze came in your direction. And you want to be there rather than at the strip, with its hot tarmac; but even more, you would maybe not want to be on the other side of the town, away from the pretty centre, where green gave way to swamp, and the fetid smell caught your nostrils in the summer.

At least that is what the ladies who lived on the best street said.

Oh sweetheart, *never ever trust the best ladies!* You do not need decorum; you'll be wanting dirt under your nails. Because in dirt and tree root integuments under fingernails and just a whiff of fetid stuff, now that is a better place to look. Yes: dirt is more beautiful than decorum.

Down by the swamp lived old John Fogle; he had, children said, the gift of second sight and, along with his cold, hostile wife, and his unfriendly brood of female offspring, did not like people to stray their way. The children were at school but chose to play together, shunning the company of Missy or Mary Lee or Claudia. Did well in school, though. Top of the class. Certainly, the other girls in the class tried hard to be friendly – the ones, that is, whose mothers had not warned them away from the Fogle girls. The ones with the kinder, more broad-minded mothers or those who wanted to rebel against their mothers, for this was also a town in which mean-mindedness and snobbishness tended to run rife. It was all the fault of the best ladies.

Today, one young girl was determined. Betty was kind but also intent on one day getting down to the house and looking more closely at the swamp. And she persisted: 'Can't I come home and play with y'all?'

'No. Pa wouldn't allow it.'

'Why not? I'd be good.'

'Don't matter.'

'Why not?'

'Nothing. Can't tell.'

Such enigmatic last answer was all she needed. It was not exactly a no. So she told her mother that she had been invited home, and her mother allowed her because she, too, was kind and kind of curious to know about this family and, essentially, believed that they would treat right if treated right. She had been looked at sideways by the best ladies and found, word-lessly, wanting. So, Betty followed. 'Go away. Pa don't like it.'

'Oh, go on. You yella?'

'No. Well, if you go away after.'

And there, in that place beyond the proper stuff, they were. Old John Fogle stood up rigid, in the grey menacing way; his eyes were mud and coal, but then, as the child held his look, came a smile, and the kid smiled back. A messy smile. And real, both. Sure, the area around the house was close to the swamp; you could smell the heavy air. But it was also toothsome and beautiful and a breath of fresh air after the tight little corner of town where Betty lived. Near, yet far away and pointing at odd things you could not see, taught fingertips at your elbow, brushing at you with a new welcome. And the house was tatty but oddly welcoming and festive. Yes, festive. A dirty Christmas or Easter run wild. Like anything could happen, and Jesus would laugh too. And Betty liked it. Gradually, the girls began to play with Betty, too. Chase and hide and go seek and anything that took their fancy. And Betty met their mother who, in a startling and untidy way, was also unexpectedly beautiful.

The girl stayed for the evening meal, too. Basic and old-fashioned, but substantial, too. And, while no one said much, Betty realised that she had been accepted. Maybe she would be able to go back. This was a place of generosity and of riches. She ate and ate, and there was always more, and her appetite was not assuaged, though, at home, she ate like a bird.

Next day in school, the Fogle girls continued to play together only, but they looked sideways at her even with a hint of a smile. She felt happy. It was, in its way, all rather mysterious. She wondered, too, why John Fogle looked so old: more like a grandfather or even a great grandfather than a father. We hear, from sensible ones, about how fetid air is bad for us, yes? Well, what about if the damp and that moist spell of a life enlivens the parched body and gives birth to new things, in old things? Ever entertained that about swamps? About the rich chew of roots and mud. No? *You lack imagination, then.* And you misunderstand horror, mistaking it for what is beauty and economy. Because John Fogle was not the girls' father, and he did have the gift of second sight. There's magic in the chew. And necessary killing, because you've got to steward the earth and what's on it for otherwise hoity-toity and mean and green will take over the world. As I was saying, Fogle not the girls' father but the girls' great grandfather, and he had, for more or less good reasons and by folks we cannot name, but the rich chew knew well, been preserved for his gifts.

Father and grandfather? Gone. To the swamp one day. John Fogle saw what they would become. Told you that old brackish water was fetid. Not just that: it lived and breathed and did what it would do. And John Fogle was its custodian, being no murdering sort himself, exactly. Betty would be simply fine because, as I told you, she was kind and looked without arrogance – only with spirit, love and curiosity at the world, in the way child and adult should. And those hoity-toity mothers who lived on the best street on the other side of the park? Well, better not go the Fogle way. Because there are things in the swamp, maybe only the clean mind of a child will welcome and understand. Not you, momma, city boy, architect of tidy things and best lady. *Betty*. You? Your Sunday glove would come floating to the surface while the dinner gong beat and people would turn away as a shimmer of a wave passed over the water and the efflorescence of old roots.

Old Age; New Blood

Flora was a funny kind of girl, struggled with friendships in school, not the sort to be able to stand up and receive a prize for anything, but, you know, bright enough – just not the sort, as she was once told, to set the world on fire. Hmm. She struggled with that one because, of course, like more than would care to admit it, she *wanted* to set the world on fire, to be conspicuously brilliant (modest, though), known to be kind, intuitive, creative. Well, and pretty, too. Shy throughout, she would smile at other people, older people especially; they looked more interesting, with their textured skin and chiaroscuro under their eyes. But it never really occurred to her that she might engage them in conversation; why would one talk to a kid? They probably had plenty of hapless, half-dead friends of their own, didn't they? Flora was dark-eyed, intense, but clumsy and the peers called her weird; back then, she did not see that being an eldritch child is better. It is more fascinating, and you can cultivate your oddity so that it breaks and burns others' pretty little things. Flora was damned by faint praise: 'We can't all be a beauty queen, and all that matters is that you try hard. You will find your place.'

Or, 'I know you're not really determined, but we're still proud of you. Your colouring is interesting, and someone will appreciate it.' *Lovely, lovely.*

She gnashed her teeth, sweet, plain unambitious little thing.

Rhoda lived down the row. She was about eighty, with a soft, kind face but, Flora sensed, girders of steel. Rhoda had had a tough life, widowed two years ago, and had lost a child in adulthood, too. There was something resilient about her; joyful, even. Plus, a hard eye, which was dark and shiny like that of Flora. For the first time, someone who was good, but with the potential for a prepossessing calumny. Flora was tired of trying to behave.

One day Rhoda asked Flora in. *I could not. Oh, she is very old. It is odd. Look at her choppy little teeth! Are they real? Her gums are the colour of candy floss and flamingos. But then they say I am the weird girl... and I like her; I really like her.* It was on a day when Flora was just kicking about in the garden, disconsolate, after a bad week at school which nothing seemed to cure, when Rhoda asked her to come and help, talk, perhaps eat with her. Flora went. Flowers needed moving, but Rhoda had stiffened up. Limber Flora felt that she would not know what to say to Rhoda but also understood that she must lend a hand, and the dark shiny eye of the old woman spoke complicity. So, flowers were moved to a better spot; clumps of irises and opium poppies were divided: Flora discovered that she knew a bit about this from having watched her father at work. Not instruction; just osmosis: being ignored and a pleasant nobody at home had its advantages. The next week, clematis and honeysuckle cut back under Rhoda's watchful eye. She could prune; she had learned that too. Flora saw, to her own delight, that she knew about finding a strong shoot and where to cut.

Getting ready for spring and the cutting back, its precision, was exhilarating.

And Rhoda gnashed her teeth, too. *How lovely.* Our young friend relaxed and began to chat. Squabbles with her more articulate, popular, profoundly more modish schoolmates began to recede with snipping, tidying, mud and the abundant cakes and cups of tea that Rhoda produced. The girl began to chat to Rhoda – about her parents, school, not being particularly good at anything. Rhoda listened, gave her the occasional pat on the arm and said simply, 'You will find your voice and, you know, when you get to my age, you'll see that none of the things you worried about ever came to much. And, of course, I can help you on the way, my little eldritch girl. We can start right now if you need. I have been hoping for someone.'

Flora is older now, surer of herself; Rhoda is further unsteady on her feet, brittle-backed, though her eye is darker and shinier. Rhoda prompts and urges in all things: composting, cutting and calumny. For assuaging loneliness cuts both ways, with the burn of old age passing to the child who cannot resist it. Sometimes the least likely person might be a peculiar girl's best friend when it matters most. If you are lucky, poor child, she will gnash her teeth with you, and you'll feel like you can go forward with a friend while those other pretties go, fresh and trimmed-up in company, down the primrose path to the eternal bonfire.

How lovely!

Any Seventh Sunday

Tom the poet sat at the back of the church. It was Pentecost, celebration of the day God sent His Spirit amongst his people. Fire, wind, comfort and inspiration for all time.

'No. I just don't get it,' he said silently to himself – not for the first time, as he sang the hymns, smiled at people about the church and tried, where appropriate, to look solemn and meditative. What is that they *see*?

'I mean, I keep coming here – I like the building; it's peaceful. But I do not *feel* what they all seem to feel. What has been revealed to them, and why has it never to me? Are they arrogant and pleased with themselves because they are so sure about their faith? I am not sure I even like that. Are they wretches? I've always disliked religious people but always wanted to be one.'

The unfunny joke. Hell is other people, but mostly it is yourself.

Tom found that, despite his best intentions, he was riled. Irritated because no one was helping him. If they were so close to God, why couldn't they sense that he was struggling? His chest felt tight. He was getting the old, frosty demons again. *Emma Gifford.* How could it have all gone so very wrong, and now she was gone, too. And here, in a place which was supposed to help him, he could find neither solace nor guidance. He had no choice but to write more poems and hope his new wife did not notice. Now, the nave laughed, the rood screen shook with its own knowing hilarity, and the flags of the floor rumbled. In the crypt, the priests, in a rubble of bones and ash, all hummed. He cast his eyes desperately around the church, hoping to see something to comfort him, but instead, the memento mori on the tombs loomed larger, closing in; deaths' heads cheering on the reminder of his death and eventual desiccation after, that is, the bit that was even more horrifying: the ravages of grave worm and the slip of clay.

'Out. *I cannot stand it. I cannot do this anymore*, skulking at the back. I need some air. I don't want to hear all this talk of the Holy Spirit coming among us. What about me? No one or nothing has come to me.' Outside, though, his breathing came deeper, and the grave worms burrowed back down. It was a warm spring day; May the twenty-third. The poet could smell the last of the cowslips, a warm honeyed breath. The lily of the valley mingled in their sweet, fresh scent and the earth, he thought, exhaled. Now, he saw the old gardener was at work, not in church. Keeping the Garden of Remembrance tidy; mowing and clipping. And always with a pickaxe to one side as this old man often helped with the graves and loved to take a swing at sod. When he saw Tom, he sat down. Mocking, smiling: 'Morning, poet.'

'Well, as you know, I write novels, too,' said Tom unnecessarily as the old man coughed up a sad chuckle. 'Church a bit stuffy for you, was it? Artistic type like you?' And Tom, without having intended to, poured out what he felt about church going. Even said some quite unpleasant things about the parishioners and some of the faithful dead. And the old man listened without comment. Finally, Tom stopped, aware that attention was waning and that, perhaps, he was being boorish on this fine spring morning when folk had gardens to tend and services at which to worship. The old man had begun to pick at the ground, scoring vertical and horizontal lines, an expert eye measuring the sod. Now, the old man stood up and turned from him, lifting his spade, fork and trug. With remarkable alacrity, shouldering his pickaxe too. Still, he said nothing. Tom worried that he had caused offence.

Damn it all and damn himself, too. 'Low born churl', Emma had once called him. Now he could add 'blasphemer', 'man with ideas above his station' and 'berater of old men going about their peaceful business'. 'I'm sorry. I did not mean for that all to come out. I can see I have caused offence,' he called after the man.

'No offence, no. But I must be going about my business. It is funny, though. You're not observant, and you're a man who writes about noticing things.' The gardener walked on and stopped, still without turning around. But if Tom could have seen his face, as we do now – that's him in the photograph – he would have seen a wry smile playing about the corners of the mouth.

'No, poet. Never you mind. I always listen. *I* notice such things. And I'll tell you this. The garden is warm today, and do you see the breeze around the flowers? Like a heat haze, isn't it now? This is my church right here. And you might want to take your jacket off and sit for a while. It is the Spirit, you see. Followed you out here. Does not stand for none of your nonsense. Came to you because you could not come yourself. Just like the priests in the crypt hummed, and the deaths' heads loomed larger. Still, you didn't catch on.'

The old man raised his pickaxe above his head in goodbye; just for a shade of a moment, Tom felt cold fear, but the man turned, and Tom was alone in the garden, save for the lingering impression of a man who was never there and his footprints a memento mori on the damp grass.

The Bookshelves of Amos Biblio

Amos Biblio, lord of all he possessed, which at the time was not all that much, felt disappointed by what he perceived as the slights and slanders of everyday life. And thus, he thought he would withdraw from life and build himself some splendid bookshelves and begin to fill those shelves with beautiful books. He had always liked carpentry and had tended to take refuge in his home and in reading when he felt things were not going well. The bookshelves provided him with an absorbing project; he was cheered by the making of excellent joints and with the odd flourish of carving at the edges of the shelves – just a subtle scroll for these times; nothing too much. As he worked, he thought about how, when the shelves were done and filled with new books, he would stay in more. After all, in his entanglements with people, he felt susceptible to critical voice. If he retreated a bit more, he would surely be happier. And in his warm, isolated state, he could stay, apart from forays to earn and invest money, until death took him. You could not trust people. Finally, he had come to that pass. And Amos could not tolerate people who would not read.

Eventually, the bookshelves were finished. One for most of the rooms of his house, all with slightly different design and, in some rooms, painted in dense and solemn colours. He gazed at his shelves and his woodworking tools and felt content, but when he looked outside the window, he felt a pang of anxiety. Oh. The outside world. Other people. Now, he assembled what books he had on the shelves and saw how empty those shelves looked. Right: he would buy his books online so as not to sully the perfection of what he had done. For what if someone looked askance at him when he was choosing his books? Then, perhaps, his project would feel spoiled. Just then, his skin was thin, and he was nauseated at the society of others. For a moment, looking at the sky, he was unsure if he could stay in bibliophilic warmth, alone, until death took him. Could it work, or did it desiccate the brain and give you a life, and death, of dry reading, however strong your will? Was the society of others to be incumbent on you?

But he brushed away the outside world and determined to find everything he needed within the pages of the books. Ah – but Amos found he could not get everything he wanted; in the second month, up bubbled isolation and a lexical sort of lust. He began to want to handle the books, to look at them as physical objects and admire their aesthetics and have them there to eat up the stories within. Greedily and rapturously. A sex-way thing. It is only natural for the bibliophile. So out he went to add to his collection. He had no Greek Myths on his shelf, for instance: how he had enjoyed listening to his father read from *The Golden Porch* when he was young. So that was the first thing he looked for. But while in the shop, time stood still, and he was reading, reading; lost in pleasure, just as another was, near to him. He looked at her sideways. Hmmmm. Helen?

The next day he went back to buy more books, and she was there again. He would tolerate the book botherers and fiddlers for her. This time she looked sideways at him and caught his look. Eventually, Amos's bookshelves were full of texts that told him not only when to be alone but also how you might live with a full heart. And then he and Helen – the face that launched six bookshelves, as it turned out – threw a book party. Perhaps, if Amos could find true readers, it would not be so bad. It could even be good. People came; they were intrigued by the strange man. They began to touch his books, even to handle or read them. *What a frontispiece! What a story! Have you read, my dear? That would not do.* Amos Biblio shivered. He watched Helen as someone fingered a spine and then bent it, crack. She dug her fingernails into her palms. It went on. The Biblios gave out champagne and put the room into whirl, moving quickly among the volumes and then whipped them from the hands of the book botherers, fiddlers and philistines and pushed those guests out into the street.

I say. Well I never. Why did they. Why didn't you.

Sober, Amos Biblio and Helen retreated to one of their library rooms and caressed then whispered to the books. It was then that an extraordinary thing happened. Things were moving, books beginning to push out here as if volumes were binary code and, gradually, more urgent as if lives depended on their argot. And the books began to whip about and whistle and whisper back to them, cuffing them here and there, judging them incompetent readers in the battening down of their kindness and the skewering of their guests. It was hard to tell which titles were angriest, but if you'd stopped time, you might have seen stately plump Buck Mulligan snarl and Ishmael saying never to call because stories want to holler and be shared; because books are fine things, yet they are not precious unshared things, to be secreted. Both needed to learn. The books spoke and spoke hard and judged them.

But did they listen? Amos Biblio and his Helen?

Look in. Can you see them there, buried under a shiny avalanche of the *Da Vinci Code*? It is the final part of their smothering. Words jump out: *The problems arise when we begin to believe literally in our own metaphors,* shout the weirdly multiplying Da Vincis. Now both Amos Bibilo and Helen want to shout, *how can you believe literally in a metaphor?* But their throats are parched and breathing scant.

What a way to go.

Amos Biblio, lord of all he possessed, which at the time was not all that much, felt disappointed by what he perceived as the slights and slanders of everyday life. So, he thought he would withdraw from life and build himself some splendid bookshelves and begin to fill those shelves with beautiful books.

Walter Muscovy and the Big Love

Walter looked a little like a duck. His nose was beaky, he had an unattractive gait which was, you have guessed it, more of a waddle, really. For a man, he was short but compensated for it with good cheer. In Walter, there was not a whiff of arrogance or the slight bitterness one sometimes sees in those who have a chip on their shoulder due to perceived misfortune. And there was one more thing: Walter was very, very funny. He had the sort of timing which would cause his friends – and he had coerced many – to double up, to have painful sides. He was also articulate without being showy. Walter loved words. Felt them in his mouth like something smooth and minty (a humbug) or rough and to be handled carefully (managed carefully with your tongue).

Walter's mother loved him dearly; to his father, he had always been a bit of disappointment, though Dad tried not to show it. Walter was clumsy, and in those who did not know him, he might cause giggling or the foolish scorn of those who really should know better but do not. Walter, also, had never had a girlfriend – but he lived in hope. Waddling on through and making people laugh.

Walter Muscovy had secrets, of course. What man has not? Secret signs and visions and songs. And thoughts of damp parlours where he tuned bosoming cellos and climaxed over bassoons, but in a pure and tuneful way and not, oh not, with the filth.

That day, on his way to work (Walter restored fine musical instruments), he had an odd sensation that today was different; an inchoate feeling – not of dread, but of a sort of warmth spreading up through him. One might say a new kind of happiness. There was a woman waiting for him at the shop; she had a cello and was tall and willowy. She had the gentle flush of the English rose and strawberry blonde hair; she wore a white coat. Almost, he dared say, a little like a swan. Walter did not mean to look a little too intently, but then she was, to his eyes, heart-meltingly lovely. But does a swan look kindly upon a duck, or does she peck at his neck and kill him for being scant, stump and in her way? Or does she start with bill and coo and end in breaking his arm with one swoop of that prodigious wingspan?

Yes, I can restore your cello to health. A cello, Madam, likes a damp parlour such as mine. It will take this long; these are the procedures I am likely to follow, and yes – it is a truly fine instrument which you're so right to treat with reverence and want to bring back to its former glory. He was avoiding her eyes for fear of blushing, but when he looked up, she was staring intently at him. There was an awkward silence. Now or never. He would not die if she laughed in his face. He imagined cooing and nuzzling the neck of this pen.

'I have a break at about eleven. I wonder if you would like to come and have coffee with me. At the new shop over the road?'

Well now. They were both blushing. She had long fingers for plucking; exactly right for pizzicato. Ooooh. Sul tasto and sul ponticello. Stop, stop, Walter Muscovy! The pen took off as if on open water, and then, later, they drank their coffee and talked and talked and the next day, too. Like him, she loved to play with words, to handle them and feel their heft. And Walter worked on the cello until he had brought it back to clear, resonant notes and a burnished beauty. She struck some notes right there in the shop, and he almost cried. But she stopped him, right there, with a kiss and the world around went silent. Yes, they do make a funny-looking couple, the swan and the duck. But they laugh constantly and make the kind of music that reverberates long. With them, you hear, you *feel*, the grace notes: those notes between notes that you take in on a visceral level. There are three little ducks or swans. They have their mother's grace and their father's waddle – a curious combination, but a good one.

But it is a risk, isn't it? Love. That he is a duck, and she is a swan. As he ages, his waddle will slow while her broad white sweep will always captivate. Overall, a sweep is always beautiful, but a waddle calcifies. At that point, will his children curse their hybridity and, in those grace notes, look askance and plan a long-beaked peck? When Walter Muscovy is a raggedy duck, will she take the bosoming cello from the damp parlour and have at it with the Elgar while the cygnets swipe and extend their wings?

Lately, this thought is keeping Walter Muscovy up at night.

Nightshade

'Will your lordship please to taste a fine Potato?
T'will advance your withered state.
Fill your Honour full of most noble itches
And make Jack dance in your Lordship's breeches.'
—John Fletcher, *The Loyal Subject*, iii, v, 1617

It may be that you have never looked properly at the common potato, but the fault lies with you. No potato has ever been common, for it has a rich and delicious history dripping in lard, butter, spice with a finesse of debauchery and a wish for more: *more of everything.* That is its nature. It is many things. And if you think the potato's only role is to be mashed to smithereens, chipped, or, if you are the sort to go out for supper parties, misrepresented in dainty coils and piped, then you ought to read on. And best, also, not to assume certain things about it or the person who tends it. Or he who has the temerity to say he knows it best! Fine: this is a dark tale, but a delicious one. Come wade through victuals and skate upon a dauphinoise with me.

My name is Belladonna, my middle name is Atropa, and I like hasselbacks, the smell of earth and extraordinary strength and fervour. I like woodcutters and potency, sex, and a fine table of celebration. I like bold funerals, colour, and fire.

I was once married to Earl Julius Clopton. I did my best by him but had to assuage myself with extracurricular passions. Nights with him were cold and mechanical, and he had the ardour of a soft, sad dish of cold whipped potato made by a nanny who had never been hot or happy. I tolerated it until I could no more. If it had not been his fault, that would have been one thing. But it *was* his fault. He could not be tempted, would not deviate. You know, there are legions of these sprauncy fellows, burying alive their glorious and intemperate wives, poor undeveloped blooms, crushing themselves and miserable, eying a hungry man for their bacon but forced to live with gammon. With a Julius Clopton, forever. It makes me shudder even now. All women should learn to poison such men.

But as I was saying. The potato, yes. It was a subject awaiting an author. The potato has had a long and colourful life. A member of the botanical family, Solanaceae, a cult of flowering plants that range from annual and perennial herbs to vines, lianas, epiphytes, shrubs, and trees. It includes agricultural crops, medicinal plants, spices, weeds, and ornamentals. Atropa belladonna, commonly known as belladonna or deadly nightshade, is a perennial herbaceous plant in the nightshade family, which includes tomatoes, potatoes, and the bold and shiny aubergine. It is native to Europe, North Africa, and Western Asia. Its distribution extends from our England to Ukraine and the Iranian province of Gilan (I may have had husbands in both those places) in the east. It is naturalised or was introduced in parts of Canada and America. Some claim that all the plants, like creatures in a cult, are damaging. This is because they have never met Atropa Belladonna.

I know best how to handle the Solanaceae. This is my family. I know that the foliage and berries are extremely toxic when ingested, for they contain tropane alkaloids. These toxins include atropine, scopolamine and hyoscyamine, causing delirium and hallucinations, and are also used as pharmaceutical anticholinergics. These tropane alkaloids appear to be common in the family Solanaceae, as they are also present in plants of the genera Brugmansia, Datura and Hyoscyamus, of the same family but in different subfamilies and tribes than the nightshade. Ah, I am botanist and chemist as well as epicure and lover. I have a large family and an obscene number of cousins.

We are bold, bold things. People are often scared of such boldness – of passion and impropriety.

More fool them. Atropa belladonna has unpredictable effects, and so does Belladonna Atropa. The antidote for belladonna poisoning is physostigmine or pilocarpine, the same as for atropine. But I do not care for antidotes other than my own antidote to life, which is cunning, and my antidote to boredom is poison, which you have likely gathered, my sweet berry reader.

The potato. What a colourful family it has! What you may think of as the common and grubby English tuber was, to our ancestors, in fact, the sweet potato: patatas, not potatoes, nightshade to your convolvulus, your – forgive me – morning glory, and it was not until quite late in the potato quaffing that the English variety replaced the Spanish Ipomoea batatas, for our stolid lot was growing to love the *Solanum tuberosum* that is such a bedrock of the gustatory experience across the land. And into it came a man, a most remarkable author. He became one of my husbands, whose name was Earl Julius Clopton. At first a doctor, his tuberculosis halted his work as Director of the Pathological Institute at the London Hospital in 1904, and he would then spend six months in a Swiss sanitorium. It took him over two years to fully recover from the illness, changing the course of his entire life. Rumour has it that his strength was gradually renewed by dishes of creamy, sieved mashed potatoes. Baby's food. That fitted him. He purchased a house in Barley, Hertfordshire and, because he could not return to practising medicine, began experimenting in the emerging science of genetics under the guidance of his friend William Bateson. After several failed experiments with guinea pigs, Monarch butterflies and hairless mice, Earl Julius Clopton decided to experiment with potatoes after seeking advice from his gardener, a man called Evan Jones, a salty and rough-handed genius from Carmarthen whom I enjoyed many times and came to admire greatly.

Evan Jones was one of those geniuses whose work is usurped by posh folk, but I held him as he wept about that, and he held me as I wept over his trugs and piles of hoes, mostly facing forward but sometimes held aloft because as well as being a potato expert, Evan Jones was a man of prodigious strength and appetite. He would be pricking out seedlings or pruning, and by God, for within minutes, there was thunderous congress and in any place. It pained me, appreciating Evan's prodigality as I did, that he had been humiliated by his master in this way.

Later in his career, commenting loudly on his decision to study potatoes, Earl Julius Clopton, my then husband, noted that he had, 'Embarked on an enterprise which, after forty years, leaves more questions unsolved than were thought at that time to exist. Whether it was mere luck or whether the potato and I were destined for life partnership, I do not know, but from that moment, my course was set, and I became ever more involved in problems associated directly or indirectly with a plant with which I had no affinity, gustatory or romantic.'

I was at a party at one of the country houses of his horrid and temperate acquaintances when I heard him say this. I often went to such parties and noted that the cold company, the women there, looked askance; gazed at my beauty, but thought I was a whore he had passed off as his wife (though I prefer the word *courtesan* and grew to hate the word *wife*.) I had more class and elan than the gentry and was lither of limb and of more prodigious imagination in bed.

Earl Julius Clopton was guffawing his potato speech to the assembled company, and while it hurt me to hear him say that he had felt no affinity, gustatory or romantic, with the potato plant, I had thought that at least he possessed some imagination and would come on in time because he looked sturdy enough. When first I had that thought, that he might *do*, I had made a play for him and, of course, succeeded, sweet poison and all and, in time, came to have exquisite rooms in his mansion in Hertfordshire. I had been wrong. He was cold and mechanical and barely bit me or looked me in the eye.

Then that eye went roving.

But here was the thing. Earl Julius Clopton learned from Evan Jones but took all the glory, and Evan Jones was angry. That made me angry. My husband's book, *On the Common Potato*, was lauded as a noble work in *The Spectator* and a work of the most extraordinary scholarship by *The Times*. On another occasion, I heard him downstairs talking to friends, peers, old duffers from the House of Lords; Evan Jones heard them too because he had shimmied up the drainpipe and clawed his way in to visit me mightily in my parlour, and there we lay. My husband was in his cups and chortling, 'No one knows as much as I do! I know more about the potato than any man living!' I saw Evan Jones set his jaw and snarl; my own eyes were wide. My husband did not appreciate the potatoes. What did he know anyway? I had looked at drafts of his magnum opus – his spelling was not so fine for a titled Cambridge man, and with a doctorate, too – and he had even failed to note that in the Renaissance, patatas meant sweet potatoes to many. They had come from Spain and, oh, roasted in ashes, a delight of sweetmeat, and do you know that some thought them like marzipan, only yet more delightful. Marzipan is a lovely thing to think about when you are in flagrante delicto.

Earl Julius Clopton was unaware of the true glory of the potato, and while he alluded to its role as an aphrodisiac, he did not ingest them in that way. His book was marvellous on the potato story, I will give him that; he'd traced the tuber's roots to the Andes and explained that it was of vital significance to the Incas, the fatal plantings, blight, a mythical connection with Virginia and confusion between the sweet potato, the Jerusalem artichoke and, would you believe, the truffle. But he would say all that because he had been tipped off by Evan Jones of Carmarthen. He was comprehensive enough on the link between luxury – which the potato was for the Tudor gentry – and sexual congress, but on the aphrodisiacal qualities, he lacked warmth and insight. I have been laughed at for suggesting that the humble potato is the greatest antecedent to powerful sexual congress, but I am correct. I add that if there were a poor harvest one year, a potato blight, tomatoes and aubergines might be explored; tomatoes are love apples, it is true, and, don't you know, applying aubergine juice to yourself as directed by the *Kama Sutra* is very effective, and I could show you some very saucy haiku about aubergines if you are passing over my divan sometime.

My then husband's noble study was published to great es-
teem, and earls, viceroys and baronets, effete potato fiddlers
all, came to our Hertfordshire home. I was in attendance then,
though yearning for Evan Jones, who had a secret sunken hot
Turkish bath project on just for me, lurking behind the com-
posters in areas where my husband never deigned to walk.

Working with the servants, I gave out witty little dishes of
whipped potato with commemorative spoons; I was a cour-
teous wife. There were crisp and soft potato croquettes and
little amusements of scalloped potato and chipped fripperies
no wider than a baby's finger. And the guests brayed and con-
gratulated their host. Later, they sat down to a full potato-
rich dinner and that, you see, is when our plan began to swing
into action as we busied ourselves crushing berries. Because
he had missed it all, you see. That it is wrong to steal and
covet the work and life's knowledge of another man, that self-
congratulation and uppity ways are appalling and may war-
rant drowning in a bowl of Vichyssoise. There is nothing quite
as revolting to a woman of my hot temper as disappointed
concupiscence, of fervour met with a tallow face and a most
poor quality of aubergine.

As I told you, my name is Belladonna, my middle name is
Atropa, and I like hasselbacks, the smell of earth and extraordinary strength and fervour. I like woodcutters and potency,
sex, and a fine table of celebration. I also like bold funerals,
colour and fire, and run to satisfy cravings for green and purple berries, things cousin to me. My husband had never even
noticed my name: it means Deadly Nightshade, and I daresay
he just thought it was pretty if a little whoreish. Evan Jones
knew, of course. *A beautiful thing that could kill you.* So that
night, after our aubergine ritual and dishes of roasted tomatoes with the hot spices he grew just for me, I added some-

thing special to my current husband's nightcap, the results of the crushing. The maid was in on it; they always are. And we put the green and black berries of the nightshade in the juice, and that was it. I thought of many things more theatrical: drowning in a barrel of potato potage or tying him to the bedhead and forcing him to feast on the eyes of many potatoes until he expired. I even thought of chopping him and putting him in a pie with an unctuous gravy made from his viscera.

But I am not a savage. Perhaps he choked a bit, but mostly he did not wake up, and I played the widow. To my delicious shame, Evan Jones from Carmarthen later cut me out of my funeral weeds with his best secateurs, and there had been another bold funeral. Soon, in a blackish ceremony, Evan Jones became my new husband. Oh, he was a hot man. But you missed the woodcutter clue, perhaps? Ah. Harold Ebsen from Deptford came to maintain the estate's woods, and with him, I found such delectation, and he was fond of my whoring and knew more about the wild plants of the hedge and woodland than Evan Jones. Harold was a man more of the shade than Evan Jones of Carmarthen, who was ruddy-faced and of the sun, like a heliotrope, or a Jerusalem artichoke, *Helianthus tuberosus*. I have never found one man to be adequate.

I am asking the question of you, my precious little berry, my sweet and murderous reader.

'*Ah*,' I sing to my bosky young lover, 'come, sweet boy. Wade through some victuals and skate on a dauphinoise with me. My name is Belladonna, my middle name is Atropa, and I like hasselbacks, the smell of earth and extraordinary strength and fervour.'

It Is Not Age That Withers Her

Clandestine House might, in other times, have been beautiful. Seen from a distance, perhaps it still was. A fine Georgian building, in a quay at the end of the Cleddau estuary in the county of Pembrokeshire in south-west Wales, with an orchard behind, the *haggard* (a horrid, horrid word for something so verdantly alive and productive) as Miss Davies called it, and flower borders and rockeries in front, all with an insolent beauty. It looked out across the little harbour and stood adjacent to the pretty Clandestine Arms, the village pub. You could hear the calls of the sea birds, smell the salty mud and listen to the cree of the curlews across the water. It was a changing land, with a whirling navy sky above it and centuries of other people's histories wrapped up in its dark heart. Yes, dark. The house was darkness visible. Miss Davies, treated cruelly other than with riches by her parents, mocked by her horrid brother and let down in love by her fiancé, had curled in upon herself.

On a Saturday afternoon, Idris Jones of Lawrenny had not appeared by her side at the altar. After some silent hours and a shaming by her parents, she retired to the house. Pulling back the linen cloths from the great table, now she looked at the tiered cake and the feast. She looked, unable to cry, then stabbed and stabbed and left the knives in and the feast to moulder. And when I first helped her in her house, odd jobs for an odd boy not conversant in the art of other boys your own age, well now, that feast was still there, growing fungus and families of spiders and other creeping things. When I had known her a while, she began to talk to me, disjointed but compelling and then, when I was nearly grown, she let me chip away at the depredation thereon until, month by month, the despotic table was cleared. And by then, she was old. The table was cleared, and she was withered, but it was not age that withered her, it was the sadness and the not being wanted.

And now, many years later, she was ancient beyond life. It was Christmas day. My own family was scant in celebration, so it was better to suffer alongside a fellow sufferer who knew me and whose sadness I shared like we were an old Welsh lyric, like we were poetry in motion. On this most festive day, her dress was navy or black, seldom changed, her eyes were deep aphotic pools, and her powdery skin pulled back tightly over once-lovely cheekbones. The room was crepuscular, but there was to be a feast, with tapers. And did I say that, though crabbed, there was in Aeres Davies the sense of a magical bad thing brooding and growing to time? I did not. I do now, and attend?

'Help me, boy.' Things were swimming, happening. I wandered in the strange house where books, many of which I read, were legion. In her library, spine open, on the floor. It was Shakespeare's *Pericles*. When I picked it up, my eye was drawn to the lines 'You shall prevail, were it to woo my daughter, for it seems you have been noble towards her.' The beloved child of the King Pericles, Marina, presumed lost at sea, breaks a heart, is found, and loved. I replaced the book on a shelf and closed a window strangely ajar in this fusty Christmas house. I touched a salt breeze and shivered. I sensed she had hopes for me and a lovely girl. Estuarial or city? Coastal or a mermaid called up? Something lost and found, like Pericles' Marina? I am jesting with you, but then you should not underestimate what is the air of the quay world and the whirling of the estuary. Or, for that matter, what lies under a creeper, moss, in a sea cave or about the islands out there in the Irish Sea.

Now, Miss Davies moved creakily towards the kitchen, and I felt her claw-fingers stroke my back. She was hardened and suffering, but she felt love for me, despite her hatred for the world. And then there was her pretty, nasty serving girl Seren, bringing the dishes and the salvers and the goose and the roasted apples and the potatoes and bread sauce and gravy and red cabbage and glasses of good things and Christmas cake and the brandy – spiked pudding with its coin and the matches and the cream and the silverware and I loved her and I loved her and I loved her and I knew I would never ever see that returned, though she would tease me and give me a sense of being hers, almost. She, too, was unhappy but wanted to break my heart because her own world had been shattered and was ever constricting further in the black and navy night world of Clandestine House and the quay. Aeres Davies had made it that way. And Seren, which is Welsh for star, had dimmed and withered like her.

The food and its salvers were luxurious, but the table was dusty; above the table, dark penumbrous strands of cobweb hung from the chandeliers, a joke of golden strands. The furniture had been moved again, leaving where floor and wall were now exposed, dim whorls of dust. Seren – star – served dinner and Miss Davies picked at it all, like a timid or sated bird – and I sensed plan. Big plan. I was ravenous, though, and could barely assuage myself. Then, from the corner of my eye, I saw them both glance at the window and heard the bolts slide at the front door, and I knew I was encased. It was not the worst thing, because you see it was like this. *Aeres* means *heiress* in Welsh, and though she loved a man deeply, when he understood what she was the heiress of, he abandoned her. Whether through disgust or fear, I cannot say. I had always sensed it: Miss Davies, the heiress of the natural magic and now, as I was old enough, I could begin to reverse some things through the love she had cultivated in me for her – and which I could not help – and for her nasty Seren, made in her own image. One I would marry: she had made me keen by scorn, and now the scorn melted: the other would be as my mother. And as I looked at them, across the table, on this Christmas day afternoon, there was resolution in all our hearts.

Now, we cleared the cobweb tendrils until the room was bright; and we bent back the shutters. And as I watched, Miss Davies became young again and sent the withering out into the world where it ravaged the man who had left her on the wedding day and, in his weakness, he went out on the sea and was sucked under by the unkind fingers of the kelp, and that was that, impacted in the sand-mire, mocked by a blenny. And Seren kissed me, and we were a trinity.

I never went back to my own house but lived forever here, in Clandestine on a quay of the Cleddau – and the cree of the curlews celebrated a place beyond time and loving but of effective and purple cruelty and what those of less imagination or less of the Cymraeg call *evil*.

My Dead Dears and I

Evans the Bodies loved his Dead Dears. He had established a thriving business in the low white farm buildings out the back of a farm on the coast road. In the past, this had been owned by a rather careless and drunken farmer with an insecure barn so that, from time, those who arrived for Evans's attention – silently, so silently – might have met with a stray cow crossing the yard or traversed cow pats, so hardly the most respectful of endings, or beginnings, as Evans saw it since he was fonder of the dead than the living and saw things backwards through his better eye. Nowadays, though, the yard was gravelled, the whitewash immaculate, the cows tidily restrained and a new farmer in residence. This man was laughed at by the locals as a hobby farmer. A man with an antique shop in Tenby who got people in to do the hard work and exhibited his cheese to great applause, although he had not really made it himself, and even his dairy herd looked askance, it was said on the coast road, because your dairy cow knew an amateur when it saw one and mocked in its cow-grunt while you flaunted your wares in front of the stove.

Still, at least our dead weren't shit-mired before they were interred, and that is important when you're exanimate. So there, in his low white buildings, worked Evans. And I went to work with him when I was older, into my teenage years, and he was an old, old man. I was a poor schoolboy, so they farmed me out on an apprenticeship as soon as they could. Technically, I should have been eighteen to be allowed to handle the dead, but we hid from the rules; I looked big and talked confidently and bluffed expertly and then Evans – at least to begin with – kept me away from the worst, most gruesome cases. He need not have done, for I saw no fear in temporal things and the sad features of a face rearranged; I saw them as the anagram of thereafter. There had been a day when I met a man I had never met before, but whom I had known forever... there had been a day when I had met this man as I was out playing in the sea cave. He brushed my arm, and the edges were... indefinite, now that is important to our story: to what is life; what is death; what is in between and roundabout. If you look carefully and spend time on your own in the sea world, you too will see him and that I promise.

But as I was saying, I worked with Evans the Bodies, learned from the master, and saw how he attended carefully to his craft. He had it all planned meticulously and liked to recite the rules of his job to himself and declaim thus to the world, should it be listening. Yet the best of the words was not really for me, but for the woman he had loved his whole life and whose own life and voice had been taken by the abruptly dead of her own. For with him worked Muffled Myfanwy. She went muffled after her husband, Philip Llewellyn, hanged himself in the shed, and then her son, Lewis the Younger. It had been the talk of the town because they loved to talk about death, and especially if it came unusually or an indigo sort of gruesome, but then the town stopped talking about it when Myfanwy went muffled because it seemed rude, then, to be yapping. Evans was in love with this quiet sad lady; Evans had *always* been in love with her and had seen his chance after the brace of fatalities because he reckoned she'd be proficient in death and also because of the being in love; she needed a distraction too. And then I was glad because I sensed something growing in me that day I met the man I'd never and always known. I thought, you see, to give them love and her a voice.

So now, Myfanwy worked alongside Evans the Bodies with the corpses, a delicate ballet, with tubes and brushes and buckets and pipes and the love of the dead that is known best to those sad with the living, or those born, or otherwise, with their feet half in the next world. He had dressed and buried her husband and son and allowed himself only to breathe, 'You should not have.' He had placed, under the hands of her brother-in-law, the schoolmaster, found in a mound of violets, a tiny bunch of the blooms with a sprig of rosemary: love, faithfulness, and remembrance. And I watched Evans and Myfanwy in the twilight shadows. Always I was there. Because he was lonely, even with his Dead Dears, and she was sad, and her voice was stilled, and I wanted to give her flight and for her to sing and cast off her own dead. And then there was the very intimacy of it: he had washed and nursed her lost son and sent him lovingly to his resting place; he had done the same for her lost husband, and even though the woman he loved was married to the man and the man had made her suffer, and his son had made her suffer, he nursed them and prepared them in death and felt their deep sadness, though he did allow himself to whisper chastisements, as I said, but also, 'I will take care of her now,' to both men. And when Llewellyn the schoolmaster, Myfanwy's brother-in-law, was found in his mound of violets, he took care to place his poetry book under the hands and, within it, though no one knew, he had pressed those violets from the mound because of how much their musky sweetness had been adored. My God, it was a banquet of death round Myfanwy's way. And she bore it well.

Now, because Evans the Bodies so loved his muffled company, he would narrate what he was doing, like a child before it learns that it does not have to describe itself in the third or fourth person. I repeat it now, to you, so that your fear of death be assuaged. And, do you not have the slightest curiosity of what might happen to you in such a parlour after your expiration? Well now, listen: thus, 'Now, Myfanwy, as you know, the first step in the embalming process of our Dead Dears is a surgical one, in which bodily fluids are removed with our special pipes and tubes and are then replaced with formaldehyde-based chemical solutions. The second step, mind, Myfanwy and as you know, Myfanwy, is cosmetic, in which the body is prepared for viewing by styling the Dead Dears' hair, applying some make-up and setting the facial features so they don't frighten their loved ones, all ghastly like. Whatever end they had, Myfanwy, we must make them look well and tidy. Mrs Morgan of the tractor accident will take a bit of work, mind, so you'll have to be cunning with the make-up and the brush, a bit of padding and a dress that they bought in the posh shop in Newcastle Emlyn.'

Between them, Evans and Myfanwy lifted the dead man onto the table, and Evans began gently sloshing from his vat of disinfectant and washed the body of Jones the Angry from Begelly. He had not been a good man; he was a mean old man, but he was lonely and hurt by the world, and Evans knew this, and when he washed, it was like a baptism. As he went, he signed the cross when he remembered and felt he should, but sometimes he went round and round like he was doodling spirals – or sometimes shooting stars, sometimes a maze. You are learning things now, I expect, oh curious. 'There we are now,

Myfanwy. Rub Mr Jones's feet. Ah now, look at the skill you do that with. I will massage and manipulate – he's a stiff one, this Dead Dear, and his muscles are hard with the rigor, so we'll have to loosen him, or he'll look like a board and won't be well for the funeral, and he'll startle the congregation. I had one once that sat up. Now, the neighbours say we should shave him, but I think he suits a bit of beard, don't you, Myfanwy? A new look for the old boy! There we are, isn't it? He is more relaxed already. I do think it is the way you do their feet, Myfanwy. It is your rare gift, Myfanwy.'

It was a strange courtship. Over the corpses and the bottles of formaldehyde and the tubes and pipes and the no-smell and the lowing of the dairy herd somewhere not so far away. And Evans loved the dead, and he loved poor sad Muffled Myfanwy, and he thought she might feel the same way, but it had not been so long since the hanging in the shed and the shuffleboard shooting in the back of the pub.

'And next, we set the facial features. He does look like a grumpy bastard, Myfanwy, but we must think well of the Dead Dears. Now, we have closed the eyes; what a marvel that skin glue is, and he was a stubborn one, Jones the Angry, so we used the flesh-coloured eye caps, all oval, see? They sit on the eye and secure the eyelid in place, and then a body cannot argue with us. See how tidy that is? I closed his mouth, and now you begin sewing his jaw shut. He will be quieter, then. That is it. Come closer. Be firm with Jones. Take the suture string through the lower jaw below the gums, do not be timid as you go up and through the gums of the top front teeth. There you are, Myfanwy, press hard with the needle; you cannot hurt Jones now, although maybe some would say he deserved it, so poke it in hard and keep going. That is it. Lovely work. You learn so well, Myfanwy. A model student. Now there you are, see, up into the right or left nostril and... no, not down – across, like this.'

As Evans the Bodies took the needle to show her, they brushed arms, and both felt a shiver and the warm smell of hope and happiness beyond the disinfectant, and then re-treated. Myfanwy looked away. He passed the needle into her hand. Rapture. 'That is it, across through the septum and into the other nostril and then back down into the mouth. Do not be shy. Push the needle like you mean it, Myfanwy. There is such strength in your hands.'

Had he gone too far? He thought perhaps the compliment was too heavy for circumstance. Did the dead man mind? It was at this point that Evans the Bodies realised that he had, on this instance, failed to perform the death-checks. Jones seemed to have been stiff and then to have loosened up nicely at Myfanwy's loving touch, but maybe that was because he was stiff with hatred in life and was never touched so gently. No, he must be good. He had submitted to the needle, so no need to palpate in the carotid artery. Evans knew that, in these modern times, people awakening on the preparation table was thought to be the province of the horror film, but he also knew that once Grim Peter from the old lighthouse (it's off Broadway, but, sweets, you have to look hard) had sat up to prevent his relieved relatives from celebrating that he was dead, how strong was his desire to catch them at it, hurl curses and deprive them of the fortune they knew he kept under the gargantuan pots of whitewash. There had barely been time for them to take the bunting down at the wake. But no, it was well. Present company did not need to be palpated or double-checked for cloudy corneas. And besides, Jones was always cloudy, always livid, barely alive in some ways. Evans looked at Myfanwy and considered her silent beauty.

'Then the two ends of suture string must be tied together. Do you have them there? Tie it neatly now and once you are sure you are secure with the jaw and he won't be dribbling, mould the mouth as you want it, now.'

Myfanwy nodded and tried to squeeze Jones's mouth into an enigmatic smile, and Evans the Bodies shifted the giant silver tank for the embalming and began, visualising the draining arteries as he went, draining the blood from the body through the veins and replacing with his embalming solution via the arteries.

'That is a thing of strange beauty. Formaldehyde, glutaraldehyde, methanol, ethanol, phenol, and water, and I like it to contain a few dyes because we do not want our Dead Dears looking like alabaster. We want them to look like they've been on holiday, Myfanwy, even if I do sometimes have to pad them out a bit, like Dewi after he was hit with the spade that time or I'll later be showing you how to do with Mrs Morgan of the tractor accident.'

Myfanwy nodded. Drip, drip, drip, gurgle. Magenta, to clear and clean. So quixotic! 'Now begin your magic, Myfanwy.'

Myfanwy was now holding a bag in front of her. Now, she applied moisturising lotion to the face, lips, and hands, then powdered Jones on his face, neck, and hands in order to make him look less dead than dead and cover up his scorn-blown blemishes, discolourations and the seer marks of illness that he had hidden, even from himself. She gently applied powder to his body: 'For secreted oils, Myfanwy, but we won't go so far as to polish up his nails like we did for the Widow Williams, what with her liking the glitz and the men. And just brush his hair. Oh, look, Myfanwy. He makes a much better dead man than a live.'

Myfanwy gesticulated. What did she mean? Ah – he saw. Jones was wearing a toupée.

'Just stick it back on, my apprentice. I have some Blu-Tack for such events. There we are. Press it down on his head. And now, Myfanwy, is there anything else of which we should take note, is it? Sometimes I do not know who the student is here and who is the apprentice. I mean to say' – again, had he gone too far? – 'that you have a gift for the Dead Dears; it is lovely to see. But, as I was saying, has he come with a list? Does he want a cross or a special book? Is there any jewellery for the deceased?'

Again, Myfanwy gesticulated. A bag in the corner of the room, by the silver vats of blood and lymph and life force and the plastic containers of phenol and formaldehyde. 'Ah, you thought of that, too. His belt with a tarnished silver buckle and the legend of his grandfather, Timothy the Nasty of Little Haven (it's on Manhattan Island but not a lot of people have heard of it, like) – oh the stories there are to tell – and photos of his cattle and his bird – she went to all the shows – and a picture of his chainsaws and a book. The Bible, of course? People like their Dead Dears to have The Bible even if they've been whores or accountants, Myfanwy.'

Evans the Bodies looked again. And, reader, you must surely feel at least delicately alive, nervy for the new knowledge of the parlour and the slab gifted to you, through me, from Evans the Bodies. And I will tell you another thing.

Now, Evans the Bodies knew that the Dead Dears released surprises. In life, we could not always tell if a man read, if he recited poetry every night or chapters from *the Mabinogi* to his nasty cat. An examined, deep and cultured life was not always revealed to the outside world, perhaps if the owner of those things felt they were more brilliant kept separate and apart, or he was ashamed because his family laughed at literature and effete, delicate things – thought them unmanly or unworthy; something for a stumbling, decadent Englishman, when here, now, should only be the simple words of command and desire, of shopping and betting, of curse and television. But Evans had seen more: old texts about the Dead Dears' hobbies: once, from a budgie fancier and potboy, Jim the Fish, he found a burgundy leather copy of *The Natural History of Cage Birds. Their Management, Habits, Foods, Diseases, Treatment, Breeding, and the Methods of Catching Them* by J.M. Bechstein, M.D. of Walterhausen in Saxony. 1812 was given as the first printing and, below an exquisite plate of a golden oriole, he was lost in time as he learned about ornamental cages and diseases called The Pip, The Rheum, costiveness and The Bloody Flux; for the consumptive cage bird, the suggested remedy was the juice of a turnip. Evans had wanted to read to the end of the book and understand its beauty and barbarism, but the Dead Dears should not wait, and no one wanted to see Jim the Fish because he had been bought from and dealt with – had the best crabs this side of the Neyland Bridge down towards the end of the Daugleddau estuary before the Irish sea rises to get you – but he had been unloved, so burial would not be halted, and he would be laid to rest, this secret bird scholar, the intimacy of which was only known to Evans. And to me, of course, who saw everything and thought I might visit the man who wrote the book to see how he cradled the oriole before he wrested it from his world.

In time. Visit Jim the Fish as a young man; Jones the Angry. Give them kindness and see what that awakened.

Now, Evans the Bodies flicked gently through the new old book belonging to the dead man on the table – and he stopped, arrested at a single page containing a poem; he thought it must

be a poem because it was smaller and narrower than the con-
tinuous writing. Things that were truncated were not descrip-
tion or stories, were they? He read the text aloud, stumbling,
to Myfanwy, all the while held in time, like Jones on the slab
under the turning pages, for reasons he did not yet compre-
hend:

But I will tell you some things of the monsters, or fish, call
them what you will, that they breed and feed in them. Pliny the
philosopher says, in the third chapter of his ninth book, that in
the Indian Sea, the fish called Balaena or Whirlpool, is so long
and broad as to take up more in length and breadth than two
acres of ground; and, of other fish, of two hundred cubits long;
and that in the river Ganges, there be Eels of thirty feet long...

'My God, Myfanwy, there is aqueous magic in this old book!
Stories of Solan geese and laughing dolphins and massive,
massive creatures. And look – I do love poetry, girl – he has
here a poem from that splendid fellow George Herbert. Priest
man he was, Montgomery on the Marches way he was born.
Descended from the same stock as the Earls of Pembroke, so
I like to think he's a Pembrokeshire lad. You know, when I
am lonely, I do read from the poetry. Look, see. I did not expect it here, but even in death, there is song, there is lyric.
Here, Mr George Herbert his divine Contemplation on God's
Providence. In the book too!

Lord! who hath praise enough, nay, who hath any?
None can express thy works, but he that knows them;
And none can know thy works, they are so many,
And so complete, but only he that owes them.

'Oh Myfanwy, who would have thought it? Oh Myfanwy,
what else is there to learn? Jones, nasty, cruel-tempered
Jones. Angry as an artful angler with his old book, a secret
gentleman and this poet divine? The discourse of rivers! How

beautiful that is! And what is there to teach you. What book should I or could I write for you, Myfanwy. What of Jones's end, now in the coffin, the casket as some call it, which contains the body if it's going to be buried or entombed or as a means of burying cremated bits, and it's a respectful and attractive way to transport the body before the burial or cremation, but you know that, my beautiful silent woman, because you know everything! Do I tell you now that we learn how coffin materials are a matter of style, for how can there be a material that can preserve a body forever and no material that will give you a better journey to the life hereafter? Oh, Myfanwy, my love, coffins are also available in alternative materials, such as bamboo, willow, woven banana leaf, and pressed cardboard, among other materials and things they call alternative materials and green things. Green, my love, my only. But there is not much call for them in these parts. Oh, but we can provide a half or full, which refers to whether the lid comes in two pieces or one piece and that in the case of a viewing, like with Jones, because his family want to know he's truly gone. So that they can drink and celebrate and go out on the boats and cheer, there will be a visitation, and there must be full because all of him will be on display for his beloveds to gloat on the Dead Dear.'

Evans the Bodies and Muffled Myfanwy hefted Jones from the embalming table to the coffin, now waiting on the trolley next to it.

It was terribly moving, all this, a dance macabre, a mortuary libretto. There is love in arid places and amongst tombs and in the deep and mossy places of our country that are melancholy eternal.

'Shift him with me, Myfanwy. I know you are strong. Do not be shy that you have the strength of ten men and ten of your husband and son who left you so alone! And him in his shed like that, above all those fine garden tools. And him in the back room of the pub like this and being found by Llinos as he was and she only just a woman and what did she know of heartbreak or gunshot? I am sorry, Myfanwy' – she was crying now – 'but I can keep it in no longer. I want to sing of what I feel and the Dead Dears I know. And I will teach you, like the only poem I know, about the pretty liners, Myfanwy, the fabric lining the inside of the coffin which is all in my catalogue – look see, I have it here – which is sold to us puncture-resistant and leak-proof, and is made from satin, or velvet and oh – how I favour the very materials and start from the prick and static of the polyester and the electricity, Myfanwy, oh – electricity indeed.'

Evans the Bodies moved a step closer to Myfanwy. 'And there are commemorative panels, which are embroidered on the interiors of the coffin lid because some like it, and a special thing called internal lift hardware, which tilts the inside of the coffin up so that in a full or open, the body may be viewed at an angle. I am the only man in this part of Pembrokeshire to have such a thing. Myfanwy, oh, Myfanwy, there is a thing in my catalogue called a memory tube, not because the dead remember, and not as if the atoms of the dirt and clay need to remember, but if we, silly living world, forget and if something should happen to the Dead Dears – should the coffin be dislodged from its space in a mausoleum or crypt, or unearthed from the ground, in apocalypse or great strife or a new housing development for people from away like that one on the Milford Road, then the identity of the Dead Dears can be easily known, and we do not have to exhume them. Exhume. Ex-hume. Ex-hale... Exquisite – oh, you smell of the sweetest summer meadow, my beautiful Myfanwy! Oh God, my God, oh Jesu and the clifftop Virgin!'

And Evans the Bodies fell at her feet and worshipped at her knees, and Jones lay silent and sewn up in his best suit. And then I, quiet boy, came forward from the twilight shadows at the edge of the room, and I said, with a commanding voice that came up from the deep, a place I was only just beginning to understand and which had been born in me the night I met the man I had never met before and always knew, now I said, 'Speak again, Myfanwy. Philip and Lewis the Younger Llewellyn want you to be free now. Speak, Myfanwy! Cry and let go, for here is love in this strange barren place.'

And the greater stop *was* loosed from Myfanwy's throat, and I think she was about to speak. And I think that, if she had, she would have said, 'Yes, Evans the Bodies, and thank you, and can you take me to chapel afterwards?' I think she would have said, '*Ynghanol ein bywyd, yr ydym yn angau,*' and wept. But you see, no. Because Evans, who loved her perpetual, well, his eyes went silver with the love, and he knew me, and the silvered-eyed said not to loose the stop for she was muffled perfection enough, and that was love.

And so he said, 'Yes, Myfanwy: to translate from the language of those eyes I loved always, yes, as we are in the midst of life we are in death, and here with the Dead Dears it is fair to say that we are in love.' And do you know, I think thereafter he was muffled, too, companionable with his darling.

There was another book that had only been seen by its owner, or nearly so, for Evans the Bodies wrote poems. Often for the Dead Dears who had no one and whose lives must, he thought, be recorded for posterity. So, in his book, the timid lady from the post office, who had customers and bread but no friends and a mother who would have tossed her out with the peelings for the pigs, became a cowslip in a warm meadow and drank deep of the sun and was happy; so a coarse and crooked man, who lived in the last house before St Brides Bay and whose children hated him but sang like larks for his money, was limned as a quiet man, skimming stones on the beach and smiling into the auroras of a coastal morning when no one knew. But Evans the Bodies was a watcher for the sad and lonely. He was a dresser of bodies, to be sure, but he also had a talent for the sad soul and the lonely. And he had always loved Myfanwy; when she was someone else's, as she laboured for and lost her child, when both times he bought her milk-white lilies and in her heart but not with voice, she said, 'Evans, there's a soft man you are,' and he cried with his back to her, as he did when she lost her husband. He put poems in the book for her, too. Imagined he was taking pictures of her, watching her written into the world all around and, as he watched the frosty lines on the windows in his cold parlour and saw the feathers and curlicues of winter, he scratched her monogram and, again, he cried, and imagined himself at a window as the beautiful ship Myfanwy his Love sailed away and thus he wrote this. I had seen it, of course, but he did not know. I had learned it by heart and whispered it into the Pembrokeshire night, whose kind tendrils carried it to her and caressed her, then softly laid waste to her sadness and silence and made her think clearly about Evans the Bodies, who loved her and always had, just so. And he would not ever leave her, for when their very mass of atoms disassembled and went off to abide in rock pools and grains of sand, he was sure that theirs would still mingle up there in the headland graves. So, it went, for her...

'I tried to show some better words to keep you here – to stall you with this simple moss-grown fool. Why, no. Do not go, Myfanwy – stay. Myfanwy, do not sail away. Myfanwy, yours, Evans, who loved you so since I first clapped eyes on you, girl, that cold night when they set off the fireworks from the castle for the Christmas lights. But I will wait a lifetime and set out fireworks when you are mine and then only.'

And so, just as Evans the Bodies knew that he must regard and revere the secrets of the dead and the stories corpses tell which were inanimate when they were quick (I mean the stories, not the corpses), well now, I tell his tale at the point when he, too, is gone. And his love. For, in the end, I dressed him and Myfanwy, too, you will know the procedure. As a grown man, I pressed violets into her hands and buried him with this book. I blessed their silence.

But in an earlier time, while Evans and Myfanwy basked in their courtship over the Dead Dears, just know that love is there in the barren place amidst the embalming pipes, sutures, and crackle of coffin bedding. You will remember now, and do not fear. No, you must not.

The Unguents of Ada Morgan

Time was when women hardly wore makeup at all. Makeup at the beginning of my time on this earth was still mostly the territory of ladies of the night, those in cabarets and on the black and white screen. Oh, call me hypocrite, but I loved to walk at florid dusk and see the shiny veneers on the tarts, a charcoal and that cerise mouth, clashing with the umber cheek. I thought it was *arresting*. Men would sneer at these women, and the *proper* women would too, but then those strange rich and calcified creatures got into face enamelling, which is to say, applying actual paint to the face. Make them smooth and white, unpopulated by crevice or undulation, but colourless, bleached embrocation. You want to look smooth and sanded, and you don't want to look like you're sunburned from a life of heaving in a field any more than you want to look as stygian as a miner or a boy-sweep. That was the idea.

I tell you what about the richies, though: to look paler, they have poisoned themselves. All that arsenic. And they nibbled on arsenic wafers too and got addicted, all in the name of beauty. There are a lot of them down here with me, and though, technically, I am of their class, they don't heft their bodies towards me because of the full-blown way I got painted. Whore-like, you see. I say to them that colour is still lovely for the eye even if you do not cover up the pox on your face or laugh discreetly to hide your snag tooth. Again, they turn, much as they can, in all the mouldering crimplene and fat padding of the catafalque days.

It is extraordinary, isn't it, that women with the blandest of husbands could not furnish their cheek with a pop of rouge for fear of looking whore? I love colour, crave it, especially in my present condition because it is rather dun or brindle around here. Before, I knew some women who used burnt match-sticks to darken their eyelashes or even a decoction of India ink, would you believe, and a crush of the geranium and poppy petals from their gardens to stain their lips. They did it like a coquette and mostly in secret until news began to seep out that just a little fandangle was acceptable. It pains me that, in our time, it was only lavender water or refined cologne which we women could wear. Why not a slop and plash of something musky and animal? Something that smelled more of the opium den or the best bed.

Now, it is whispered that we can use a dark pencil to elon-gate the eye and an eyelash curler to accentuate the lashes. I hear a low rumble that eyebrow darkeners have moved on from those created from gum arabic, Indian ink, and rosewa-ter, and, of course, you don't need to be Sarah Bernhardt or a dancer in the Ballet Ruse to have a full pop of a harlequin face. I am glad, glad, glad. Sometimes, in my above days, we painted in secret, so then, when it was my time, I wanted it done right. I wanted unguents on my skin, plumped up and dewy, after a gentle cleanse; I wanted a full face and a hair braid, more jewellery than, in my obedient life, I was like to wear. A dress that was outré to match, like a nightgown and soignée over my shoulder. I knew that our family would hang a wreath of laurel and yew or boxwood, tied with black crepe or ribbons, on the front door as a signal to neighbours and visitors that a death had occurred. I knew that the bell knob or door handle would also be draped with black crepe and tied with a ribbon, and I made my wishes known as a riposte to my bland husband. I said, in considering the unguents I wanted and the colours I craved, 'Put cobalt trimmings on our house and Prussian blue and incarnadine what you will, dear,' and he said, 'That I will not. Oh, Ada, silly Ada!' And I said, 'You will regret that, husband, Mr Morgan, poor colourless devil,' and began my rattle right then largely to irritate.

Now, I am glad that the gloop and the glow grew into life, and I hear rumours from up above that these days, everyone uses the unguents. It makes me feel less alone as I lie here, burnished, and furnished, feeling glad for your tincture – and hoping my bland widower is not interred with me.

ACKNOWLEDGEMENTS

With all my heart, to my husband Ned, and to my boys. Elijah, Isaac and Caleb. I hope you, my darlings, are not too horrified by the lugubrious content of this book. Especially to Kate Johnson, my wonderful agent at Wolf Literary New York. Kate has been responsible for a growth in confidence, direction and healing after disappointment, all of which she knows. Thank you to wonderful Dave at Reflex for looking after this strange little book. And massive love to all my pals. Finally, in memory of my spectacular grandmothers Florence and Beth.

REFLEX PRESS

Reflex Press is an independent publisher based in Abingdon, Oxfordshire, committed to publishing bold and innovative books by emerging authors from across the UK and beyond.

Since our inception in 2018, we have published award-winning short story collections, flash fiction anthologies, and novella-length fiction.

www.reflex.press
@reflexfiction